BOOK THREE
ST. BLAIR: CHILDREN OF THE NIGHT SERIES

THE DIARY OF ST. BLAIR

E. W. SKINNER

For Dad,

*Whose strong faith and love for God
I will carry with me forever,*

I love you.

*It is with great excitement that we reintroduce
the printed word in the year 2204*

THE DIARY OF ST. BLAIR

First publication 9/14/2204

INTRODUCTION

by Sybille Malone Cote

This is my first written work as well as *our* world's first published manuscript since the abolition of all books in 2100.

Before you start reading her diary, I'd like to share a little bit about my friend, a heavenly saint named Blair Carlisle.

As you read her diary entries, remember she only wanted to be a teenager first and foremost and to spend time with her friends. Blair was gifted with wisdom, insight, inner acceptance and the ability to see and communicate supernaturally.

She was, like many of us, resistant to share her talents, not knowing for certain if these gifts would indeed benefit others.

This frustrated the Archangel Michael, because she kept him waiting. Waiting until she was ready to write down the visions.

Michael's patience was in short supply.

Being THE warrior angel, he had divine messages to deliver, people to protect, events to orchestrate and demons to slay. But he also understood that teenagers are often chosen and need time to develop into the great saints they are destined to be.

I have learned that Blair, like Joseph—who was sold into slavery, Miriam—who instigated her baby brother Moses' protection, Moses himself—who eventually led Israel out of slavery, David—who fought Goliath, and Mary—who divinely carried the child Jesus, were predestined as young people to protect others and advance the faith.

While some of the religious leaders of Blair's time doubted her, her faith community and her parents believed in her, though they really didn't understand the supernatural insights God bestowed upon her.

In time, Blair would recognize that she had no peer in the living.

However, the mystery that is Blair—where to begin? I see her only in the dimension of her youth, when she wrote her diary.

Who Blair became after is not mine to know or see. She is a mystery in that sense. I truly hope to learn more about the person she became—the rest of her story.

There is so much buried in the rubble of our cities and vast amounts of electronic information that perhaps we'll never know.

Is that God's will?

To only know as much as is needed for our existence.

It is my hope this book will invite others to find value in their gifts, be benevolent with each other and share their talents with the world.

I almost didn't.

I am so grateful Blair still comes back to intercede for me.

She tells me that the Lord is always watching over us.

I am ever grateful that Michael and the Powers of Heaven freed us from the demons.

The demons are never far, Blair tells me. They await our weakness and doubt. They look for cracks in our armor and encourage us to fight.

They want us to believe in ourselves rather than the God of heaven. Because believing in ourselves means we don't need God or his heavenly agents—the angels and saints.

The demons want us to fail, so that we will despise our shortcomings and become emotionally, physically and spiritually weak.

Sick.

If we forget God, we won't ask for his mercy.

This *new* world is now tolerable because we know the saints and the powers of heaven. We had no understanding of mercy, forgiveness or sin before the Great Battle.

And *change* has also provided us great freedom.

I am blessed that God's Holy Spirit dwells within me and carried me through the Great Battle.

Blair and Michael baptized me after the Battle and I have a new name.

I in turn have baptized others and will continue the rite.

Blair told me that in being sealed with the Spirit or confirmed, we should choose a saint's name that we identify with or most want to be like.

I chose Blair.

I am now Blair.

BLAIR'S DIARY AND VISION AS RECORDED FROM 2004 TO 2008

BY BLAIR CARLISLE

BLAIR AT AGE 13

April 18, 2004

Today is my birthday. Well, I was born in 1991.

My mom got cupcakes at the grocery and we had pizza for dinner. My Anny gave me this diary to write in. She said someday it will be fun to look back at the things I wrote when I was young.

We are going to Disney World Friday after school and spending the weekend in Orlando.

I love Space Mountain and the Haunted Mansion best.

I didn't want my friends to go, because some of them don't all get along and it is hard to invite one without the others.

Someone always gets jealous or possessive claiming to be my 'best friend'.

I just told my parents I would have a sleepover with my friends the following weekend.

It is way easier to have friends for one night than out of town for several nights. Some are bratty for attention.

Besides, it will help my parents save money so they can get me the XBOX 360 I want!

April 19, 2004

I guess I should write about this.

I recently started having visions of people caught up in the sky. I've had others, but not like these.

It might sound like stress, but I have moments where I feel teleported to another time where these things are happening.

I don't do drugs or drink and I think I'm emotionally stable, but I guess that could be debated by others.

Anyway, it is super scary to find yourself in another time, even if only a second.

I call them God-flashes.

I totally freaked out the first time it happened.

I was 12.

It was like a test.

The frequency has picked up.

But the very first time felt like infinity. I didn't think I would ever see my parents again. I was in my bedroom one minute and in a tunnel the next.

I could hear the laugh of someone very crazy and felt a wintery wind blow over me—then, I was back in my room.

I shivered for an hour!

I didn't want to go back to that place EVER! I didn't tell my mother then.

I just held it in, *that first time.*

The God-flash itself feels like it could be a spark in creation, like a shooting star.

Strangely beautiful, but extremely frightening.

I read that falling stars are really meteorites that burn up entering the earth's atmosphere.

I hope I don't burn up on reentry of a God-flash!

It's not like lightning or anything, it is just a burst of time.

That's what it is like for me. I'm flashing between dimensions and I keep seeing this girl and I have finally learned her name, Sybille.

The name came through as Oracle. But Sybille means oracle or prophetess. I looked it up.

I can go weeks without a vision and then suddenly I see Sybille.

It is like a timer is set and when I'm just about to understand… it is over.

April 20, 2004

Ok, after writing yesterday's entry and rereading it, I thought maybe there is something seriously wrong with me. Like my brain.

I told my Mom a little, thinking she'd take me to a shrink who would prescribe a pill that would stop it.

But instead, she says, "Oh yeah, you've been talking about these things since you were very young. I think we should ask our priest for guidance."

I'm like, *What?*

Then I wondered am I crazy because my Mom's crazy?

But I don't want other people to think my Mom is crazy, so I'm just going to keep it to myself. I think.

But now I'd like to figure out if I was God-flashing as a toddler or baby and I just didn't know any better?

Like perhaps my imaginary friends are not imaginary, but real children in other periods of time?

Could we meet others who flash into our world?

Anyway, it is a relief that I can talk to mom, but she really can't help me.

She's not like most mothers, because all the stuff I tell her, she acts like it is normal.

Though I know it isn't.

Maybe we're all crazy?

Dad doesn't seem phased by mom's faith talk.

Mom said that our Catholic faith isn't unusual, but to people who have no faith, it might sound super weird.

When I was real little, mom and dad read me stories from the Lives of the Saints. Not fairy tales or bedtime classics. (Had to find those for myself, thank you very much!)

It turns out that many religious people had visions, too. The Saints.

Well, there are also many wild stories in the Bible.

It's not like I'm building an Ark or seeing the parting of the Red Sea.

Wait.

Or is it?

May 21, 2004

I need to write this down. How I met St. Michael The Archangel.

Yes, the one in the Bible. It happened last year.

I have always felt his presence.

I thought he was my guardian angel, but Michael assures me he was guarding us both!

My poor guardian angel was in Michael's shadow.

But, I guess that is a good thing.

Anyway, Michael is a force that moves things. He's too powerful to just guard me.

He's a sweeping presence. He literally moves things. Now don't conjure up ghost images, he is not like that. I unfortunately learned the difference.

(Long story.)

Anyway, it happened when I was in my bedroom after school—doing homework.

I was in bed. Books all around me. My notebook open. Pencil in hand.

A vision startled me.

It wasn't like a headache or migraine, I don't think. I've never had a migraine, so I'm not sure.

It felt like an electrical jolt to all my nerves.

I felt momentarily paralyzed and the walls shook.

I saw him in a fog.

I wanted to scream, but had no voice. I remember thinking, *am I breathing?*

It wasn't like catching your breath in a fall. My mind and lungs were on pause.

I passed out.

Then I heard a knock at my door.

It was my mother.

I heard the door open. It has a familiar whine.

Mom asked "was that my imagination? Did you feel that?"

I was partially conscious. Unable to respond. Eyes closed.

Mom thought I was asleep, well I looked like I was asleep and then I heard the door squeak closed.

Then my eyes opened and I lifted my head.

Michael was standing there with a finger to his lips, as if to say, stay quiet.

I dropped my head back to the pillow and just thought—*for real!?!? Like I have a choice!*

I rolled my head to look again and he was still there.

I didn't speak, but in my mind, I was saying—*who?*

He told me!

"It is I, Michael. We have work to do."

I then rolled over on top of my text books and pulled the cover over my head.

I wasn't going to move until he was gone.

HE may have work to do, but he could count me out!

I stayed like that for what seemed like an hour.

The corner of my history book jammed into my ribs, but I wasn't about to move.

WE have work to do?
No!
I didn't need God-flashes and this archangel, too.
He departed while I was freaking out.

June 11, 2004

It is summer and I'm totally bored. I'm helping my dad organize the garage so mom will stop nagging him. He's a clutter kind of guy.

As I was sweeping I found a pile of white powder under a shelf and I asked my dad what it was.

He said, "It's lime. A mouse died there, so it cuts down on the odor."

As I swept, I found the small bones underneath.

My mom is right! Dad needs to be way more proactive in getting rid of clutter. YUK!

July 13, 2004

Michael (THE angel) showed up at the library. I'll explain more about him later. Anyway, I was walking through the kids' section and he was sitting in on story time.

I thought at first it was a statue of him. Then he looked at me and waved.

I waved back.

My friend Mo asked who I was waving at. I then realized I could see Michael, but Mo couldn't.

I punched Mo in the arm and said, "Made ya look."

Mo rolled his eyes then went on to the new release section.

I went to story time to see what Michael was listening to.

Anyway, the librarian was reading Charlotte's Web.

I love that book!

Michael scooted down so I could sit next to him on the bench.

He said, "This is a clever story. The spider uses her web to write messages that save the pig's life."

I nodded.

"You have a similar mission," he said.

I stared at him.

He then said my job was to write in detail the vision I have for the future.

I was freaking out. How did he know about the visions?

"It will help save lives," Michael said.

I rolled my eyes.

Michael whispered, "You're the spider."

I said audibly, "Then who is Wilbur?"

The reader lady stopped and said, "He's a pig. Please pay attention and don't interrupt."

I gave Michael a dirty look.

He smiled and left. He's such a brat!

August 29, 2004

I haven't mentioned that I'm an altar server at my parish. I had a calling to do this as a very little girl.

It was about the time my parents told me that I was a four-year-old show stopper at mass.

I don't really remember that.

But I do remember watching the kids that were helping the priest during mass.

My Mom said I was mesmerized by the kids.

The church was singing "Holy God, We Praise Thy Name" and I kept singing after the second verse, so the music ministry played through all the verses and the people joined in, but softly, so my voice was heard Mom said.

Mom said that everyone was congratulating her and dad on teaching 4-year-old me so much.

Which they didn't.

I can't tell you how or why I knew the hymn, nor can my parents.

But the altar servers, a brother and sister team working that mass came over to me afterward and said I was a really good singer.

They were like celebrities to me, so I asked if I could help them the next Sunday.

They told me I had to be in second grade and go to classes to learn how to be an altar server.

I was hooked!

I couldn't wait until I had finished second grade.

And because of my excitement, everyone knew I wanted to be an altar server.

Well, the year I became an altar server was kind of ridiculous.

A lot of parishioners came to my first mass. I would say they were more excited for me than I was myself, but that really isn't possible.

Seeing the mass from the altar is so different. It is backwards. I like the ritual. However, I prefer to altar serve alone vs. with another server.

I'm a bit of a control freak I'll admit.

That first mass was hard to focus with people waving at me.

They are not supposed to do that. They are supposed to be praying and worshiping.

When I watch people come forward for communion, I think about them approaching the gates of heaven. I wonder if the verse Matthew 20:16 is true? "The last will be first and the first will be last: for many will be called, but few chosen."

From the altar Heaven seems real.

BLAIR AT AGE 14

February 10, 2005

I have no grandpas. I have grandmothers on both sides. My mother's mother and her mother are in town visiting. They are staying in my bedroom and I am sleeping on the sofa. They argue a lot.

Complaining, really.

My grandmother is my Granny and my great grandmother is my Anny.

I named them when I was little.

My Anny's name is not Annie, it is Betty. And my Granny is Lana. My dad's mother is just Grandma Iris.

My friends call their grandparents weird names too, like Meme, Gagga, Noni, and Gram.

Anyway, Anny is a super Catholic!

We all must say the rosary with her every morning when we are visiting. Well, except my dad.

Anny is very old-school.

She believes men are like God. You let them do whatever they want.

Anny's been saying the rosary her whole life and my Mom gets up super early so she can sneak out before Anny gets up.

I like the rosary.

Today is Thursday and you recite the luminous mysteries on Thursdays. I like the luminous mysteries the most. They are like when Jesus turns water into wine, his first miracle... and there are five miracles, including the Transfiguration, which is way too much to explain.

Monday, you say the joyful mysteries as part of the rosary, then there are days for the sorrowful and glorious mysteries.

Mom's totally missed the point of these prayers because I asked her which mysteries she likes and she said Perry Mason.

She wasn't joking and she wasn't paying attention either.

My mom is a little strange because she takes credit for my faith. I think she thinks she did a good job raising me—because she gets way too excited when we have discussions about faith. But not so much about her own faith.

Which puts pressure on me to keep *her* focused!

It doesn't make sense.

Mom is into faith talk. Not faith walk. That's what I think.

Anyway, Anny has a wonderful rhythm in the way she says the rosary.

I see the different scenes in Jesus' life as she goes through the mysteries.

I am really going to miss her when she goes home. My Granny and my Mom both snuck off again before rosary this morning.

It was just me and Anny and that was cool. Anny gets intense at times and the tears just flow. Then that makes me cry and I don't cry much.

More about Anny later.

April 24, 2005

Ok, the weirdest thing EVER happened yesterday. Just remember that it was a bright sunny day and not a chance of rain.

I can't explain it.

I was a speaker for youth ministry and I was to announce a retreat to recruit more teens to sign up.

Well, I had a script and everything! Father Murphy doesn't want people to talk at mass if they don't have an approved script and the length is limited to 3 minutes.

I don't mind reading from a script, I just go with the flow. Let's just say, the spirit moved me.

I got way off track.

What spirit you ask?

It was Paul, yes <u>St</u>. Paul.

He was famous for speaking to the churches in Corinth, Galatia, Ephesus, etc.

Well, I got up to do my witness and invitation and I had the paper with me and it was like a time warp happened, or something.

The closer I got to the podium. I kinda felt like I was going to pass out. I wasn't nervous. Really, I WASN'T.

But from the time I got near the altar I wasn't in control.

When I got to the podium I looked at everyone. The church was full at 8 am. This was the first mass I was to speak at and Father Murphy was saying this mass.

We have three masses on Sunday and I was to speak at each.

The 8 am was the family mass and afterwards a full pancake breakfast was served at 9 am so I was already thinking about the butter and syrup.

When I opened my mouth to speak it all began: "Grace to you and peace from God our Father and the Lord Jesus Christ."

I looked at the paper and that wasn't written down.

I spoke again: "Brethren, by the name of our Lord Jesus Christ, I warn you that a storm is coming." I looked at the crowd and I could see confused looks, but my Mom was smiling, like... *you go, girl!*

"A storm that will cause division among you and yours. Many who have much will lose their homes and become poor. The poor will be lifted up and exalted in due time. But the storm has been brewing and you are in the eye of the storm now. Please open your hearts and homes to those who are suffering that you may not suffer."

Father Murphy jogged over and slapped his hand on the microphone and it made that loud squeal.

This kinda snapped us out of the moment.

He pulled the microphone away from me, toward himself. "Thank you, Blair. Not sure what that was about, but our youth are very passionate. Her message was supposed to invite the youth on a Summer Retreat, so all teens ages 14 and up please sign up in fellowshi..."

Then a sudden clap of thunder shut the microphone and electric off before he could finish. Father was irritated, but the parishioners were looking up at the skylight that went black as a storm began **at that moment!** It was a sunny day and turned into, like, tornado-weather rapidly.

Father was talking as loud as he could but he couldn't be heard over the hail that rained down on the skylight and pelted the windows. His anger with me totally distracted him from the weather.

Father nudged me away and I was glad to move on, but I knew this wasn't going to be the end of Paul.

Some of the parishioners were urging Father to "let the girl speak, can't you see what's happening? It's a storm!"

But Father was determined to continue services and ran to the back of the building to get the battery power on. People were talking loudly amongst themselves and the noise level in the church was growing. No one was pleased with what had happened. When Father returned, people were standing and pointing at me to get back up and finish what I was saying. Father asked everyone to stand for the prayers of the faithful, which got mixed groans.

I had to go pee by then and I crept out and just stayed in the bathroom until mass was over. The rain made for a long departure for many and what I didn't know was everyone was looking for me. When I finally came out of the bathroom Father, my parents and some of the elders were waiting. I opened the bathroom door to a crowd. I guess that's what it must feel like to have the paparazzi chasing you?

"What prompted that Blair?" Father asked.

"I don't know," I said.

One man said my speech sounded like St. Paul's writing.

I said, "yeah, Paul."

Father said, "yeah, Paul. What does that mean?"

"OK, it was Paul."

My mother jumped in between all of us and just grabbed my hand. "It's time to go."

She knew this wasn't the time to share my spiritual relationships. She was the only one who understood what I was experiencing, even more so than my dad. My dad just thought it was my imagination, though he didn't doubt my spirituality, he had a difficult time embracing these events.

Father Murphy stopped Mom. "Let's finish this."

Everyone stood there staring at me. I knew this was my chance to get it over with.

"We're going to experience a worldwide famine, that's what Paul wanted you to know."

Father rolled his eyes. An elderly visiting nun, small and frail like Mother Theresa grabbed my hand and asked me to pray for mercy for those who will suffer.

"I do, sister," I said.

She closed her eyes, dropped to her knees and began the Our Father. Then everyone was on their knees saying it and I passed out.

When I woke up I was in the church office and I felt like Dorothy in the Wizard of Oz at the end, looking at familiar faces. I understood the theme of that movie too well, I really wanted to go home! But instead I had paramedics checking me. They found nothing wrong and asked if I would go with them to the hospital to make sure I was okay. All I could think was: I am never going to live this down. Father will always have his eye on me! But I guess that is what God wants, some way to get Father Murphy's attention.

April 27, 2005

The church secretary called my mother to arrange for me to meet with a spiritual adviser. It is not like a counselor. It is a person who can help assist with spiritual matters.

Spiritual matters!

OK, I am not sure these church people really get the whole supernatural thing. Because if I were to mention what I've seen, they'd lock me up.

Seriously, I don't want the attention of anyone, not the church people, the angels or the *dark side* (I don't want to say it and wake them).

If I'm gifted, why won't people listen?

If I'm not, why won't they leave me alone?

No one wants to talk about prophesy. I think my gift is prophesy. I looked it up and St. Thomas Aquinas writes there are different kinds.

I'm seriously not sure why our faith has to be so complicated.

Things should be simple like cats.

There are wild and domesticated, but who cares beyond that? Sure, there are different breeds of wild and domesticated, but that's about it.

With Christians, it should be as simple as believers and believers with gifts. Instead, we have Catholics and pretty much all the churches that developed because of the reformation. Everyone has a little different spin on the bible and how believers are supposed to live their lives.

I'm not calling myself a prophet.

I am just saying, if God thinks I need a persuasive archangel on my case... and some saints... then... I don't know, maybe I have a gift?

May 1, 2005

Before mass started today, the greeter announced that Father Murphy was the presider and everyone grumbled. I was really surprised.

I heard that the pastoral council and some of the other committees wanted to discuss the "storm" incident with Father Murphy and he said that they needed to discern if they are trying to create a storm of dissension among their fellow parishioners.

So, a group asked to meet at the diocese with Bishop Wright's office. I don't know much more than that, but I've been pulled from altar serving for the next month.

I'm to maintain a low profile until everyone gets back to normal. The parish office told my mother that I should refrain from sharing any wild idea that God is talking to me.

Makes you wonder about people, doesn't it?

I've never said God was talking to me, so it is obvious that rumors are spreading and our family may rotate to attend different mass times, so people will stop talking.

Gee, I'm not Moses.

I didn't talk to a burning bush!

But if I do, I'll likely still be told to keep the crazy notion to myself.

May 18, 2005

OK, so I met my spiritual adviser today, Sister Josephine. She is really sweet. Soft spoken. She first shared her story with me.

She is so plain.

Her skin is flaky and she isn't old. She doesn't wear makeup or lotion it seems.

I think she is my Mom's age.

Her hair is short, brunette. Her uniform is a tan shirt dress with two pockets and a thin belt at the waist.

Anyway, Sister Josephine became a nun/religious woman after she realized she didn't agree with the company she worked for. She was an executive, faithful to her job and God.

She said she was a slave to her job. She always ate lunch while working and kept to herself. She didn't go out much as she worked long hours. She never decorated her condo as she traveled for work and was never home.

But she did have a closet wonderland that was like a mini-boutique with a vanity, makeup station, organized suits, running clothes, shelves of shoes, briefcases, handbags, belts and scarves, with costume jewelry filling several cases to compliment the colors of her wardrobe. Plus, she had a dress form and a chaise.

This was her favorite place to be. She loved to organize and accessorize her clothing.

Dressing for work or travel was obviously once the highlight of her day. Strange she doesn't wear makeup or dress colorfully anymore.

She said she never felt appreciated for her mind and the closet was her safe place.

When she lost her job for blowing the whistle on others' dishonest practices, she had plenty of money saved, but no friends.

She said she struggled to find purpose in her life.

The closet soon became a museum of her old existence.

Her faith took her out to the streets. She invited many homeless people to live with her.

Up to 40 people moved in and then she got kicked out of her building, because it was against the rules.

It seemed that no matter what good she did, she was rejected.

It was bold and insane, Bishop Wright told her.

She could have bought several apartment complexes and moved the poor into them, but she wanted to be one of them!?

Jo had the intelligence to educate, tutor and assist people in legal matters, but she wanted to see the world from their eyes, she said.

The bishop asked her, perhaps God was calling her to the religious life.

It took a while but she finally concluded that her material possessions didn't make her happy and she wanted to become a nun.

She lived under an expressway with mostly men to begin with while she was discerning. She encouraged homeless women to move into shelters.

Jo was never harmed, but she did beg on the streets though she didn't need the money.

Money, Sr. Jo said, was just a tool to connect those with means to those without.

The means aren't what we think, she said.

The means are our inner gifts that the less fortunate share with us.

The less fortunate appreciate the smallest kindness of a few cents, a smile or a kind word. They bless us for giving them the smallest portion of our abundance. They are the true believers.

Jo said she often kissed the hands of the givers, which didn't go over well sometimes.

All the while her bank accounts grew.

She was a very wealthy woman living in squalor.

Bishop Wright tracked her down after hearing stories from parishioners. He spent an evening in prayer with Jo and her companions.

He demanded she come off the streets, work in the Free Clinic and see what health and wellness look like for the poor who got real help.

Sister Jo then moved into a room in a boarding house, which is where I visited her.

It is basic. She has a bed with a lamp and night stand, a writing desk and chair, plus a small television on her dresser.

She also has two chairs with a table between them and a candle on the table, a bible and pictures of saints on the wall.

A crucifix and a plaque with the word *anima* hang over her bed. I had to look that up. I didn't want to ask her. I am stubborn like that.

Anima means soul.

Sister Josephine watches me the whole time I speak.

At one point Sister Josephine said, "your mother knows you have a gift. She isn't trying to hurt you by assuming you can handle it, but she knows you are strong."

I wanted to scream. "Why am I strong? I'm the teenager!"

I also wanted to ask what "it" is? But again, I didn't ask.

That might have been the smartest question.

But I knew she was right.

I don't cry the way Mom does.

I do feel sadness and there are times when I cry, but I know God is shielding me somehow.

I feel alien because I don't get emotional.

I want to be close to my friends, eat, hang out, but I don't feel the need for relationships as other teens do. I listen to their problems and pain, but I don't share mine.

I sometimes wonder if I am a real person. I am not depressed, stressed or lovesick. No one would get me if I really shared my heart. I know this life is a dress rehearsal and that there is more on the other side.

But, what is the other side? Heaven? The real earth? Another dimension?

I feel the presence of other beings wherever I go. Most often, I know things shortly before they happen. That's how I know it's me and God working through the day.

I have my mind's picture of the future, which would scare most people. But my visions are so far in the future—I'll never know if it's accurate.

Or will I? Maybe that's the place I am rehearsing for? Could it be? I'll write more the next time I talk with Sr. Jo.

May 25, 2005

Today was a total bummer.

I thought about my meeting with Jo and my diary entry. I think I'm going to try being like my friends. Whiny. Not really, but I'm trying to understand this.

I'm always listening to everyone else's problems and the minute I start to talk about a subject important to me, my friends don't have time.

I'm serious.

I wanted to know what everyone is doing over the summer. Try some new things. I was thinking of being a volunteer at a camp or the SPCA. However, no one wants to say anything.

Don't they want to be with me?

Am I a joke to them? It really hurts my feelings when they just shut me down.

I think they are all selfish!!

May 27, 2005

My mother is driving me crazy.

She wants to enroll me in a Catholic school next year. I told her I'd run away and become a Satan worshiper if she did.

It is not that Catholic schools are bad. But I don't want to be in a school with a bunch of kids who don't want to be there either.

I mean, I have faith.

I totally get why she is wanting to do this. She probably thinks I'm going to get bullied at public school at some point.

But hey, I'd make the religious at a Catholic school mad.

I'm the one who would challenge the nuns and priests. I'm the one who sees everything differently. That's what Father Murphy and my religious education teachers say.

When they don't have an answer for me they either say, "Let me get back to you on that" or "Interesting..."

I told my Mom I'm already Catholic, and altar serving.

I'm her kid, but I am me.

Mom needs to chill.

She thinks she is protecting me or something.

If anything, she's going to get me into trouble, because I'm not going with the flow.

I want to be with regular kids and go to a regular school. Let's face it, I'm not a regular kid.

I don't know why, but if I have a gift, the regular kids might need me?

I mean seriously, look at the bible. Jesus chose a bunch of guys who were not all religious to be his disciples.

They were terrible examples.

They were excited and then terrified. They sold him for silver and denied him and doubted. Yet, he still knew they were trustworthy, because humans make mistakes.

Plus, that's true friendship!

Being able to forgive mistakes.

Okay, that makes me sound like I think I'm Jesus and that is not what I'm saying... I don't know what I mean, but I'm not trying to make myself important.

My mother needs to get out more, stop worrying and focus on herself.

July 21, 2005

My Granny moved to Florida so she could put Anny in an assisted living home.

Anny took it better than Granny.

Granny feels she has let Anny down and Anny is happy to be in a place "that takes better care of me" than Granny did.

Granny doesn't know Anny said this to me.

But Anny said that Granny didn't take her to the doctor as much as she thought she should. That's how her health declined. Anny also said that Granny should probably move in to the ALF with her, because they both need help.

But Granny doesn't think she needs help.

Anny said that Granny always gets her way. I don't know who to believe.

Mom told me that Granny is just burned out from all the years of caring for Anny. They are both high-maintenance, mom said, and they burn each other out.

The facility Anny lives at is next to our church. So now I can stop in after school and play rummy with Anny.

Anny is a rummy whiz!

I love playing cards with her.

Anny's ALF friends all gather around us and watch. It's like a tennis match and our audience sits around the table and observes our game.

So far, her friends won't play, they like to watch. They also admit they can't remember how to play and fear they'll waste our time.

I asked Anny if there was anything about the ALF that bothered her. She said no. However, she did say that two people died in the first week, and they were ancient.

Anny thinks that people in their 90s are ancient, because she is only in her 80s.

Oh, Granny is <u>my</u> new roommate—until she finds a condo to buy and moves out. She snores a lot and she is very hurt if I don't share the room with her.

We each have a twin bed.

I would rather sleep on the couch, but Granny cries if I ask to sleep in the den.

If I fall asleep on the couch watching TV she understands.

But to keep me from staying in the den, she put her little black and white television in my bedroom so I can watch TV in bed.

Now I understand what Anny means about Granny getting her way.

I just pray Granny gets a place before schools starts.

Sept 7, 2005

I hate math. I can't seem to focus on my homework. It is so annoying!

I always start doodling during my homework and then I fall asleep and nothing gets done.

I am going to fail math, I just know it.

I am writing this instead of doing my algebra.

Math is important—if you know enough, it helps you avoid getting ripped off.

Math isn't lame like history. History is just old facts and the Mayflower, the Indians and Thanksgiving. Why do we care about history?

People say history repeats itself.

Does it?

Is there going to be a revolution where people come to our country and start a whole new world?

Another Revolutionary War?

Well, I guess the Civil War was the battle within.

So, let me get this straight, we fought for our freedom from England, only to fight each other over North and South territories to create another country, the south?

But really, it was to decide if slavery would continue or end. The north didn't want to own people and the south wanted free labor.

So, people kill each other to decide which side wins?

I'm still confused about war.

The side that wins is the one who kills the most people, right? Then their law becomes the law for everyone.

That is so messed up!

Does that concept work? I guess I really don't want to know.

And these are adults running the country!

Adults telling kids how to behave and be respectful and they can't do it themselves?

OK. History can repeat itself. There is a war going on somewhere all the time.

We do make the same mistakes.

But we can also do better!

Or worse?

Argh! I still don't get math.

Kids should rule the world.

That's why Jesus said to be nice to children and the kingdom of heaven is theirs.

Whoa.

I just got that.

November 9, 2005

I called my friend Patty who is on the basketball team to see if she wanted to shoot hoops. Patty said no, her Mom is upset by the news. Patty's dad works for Central Command in Tampa and they haven't heard from him. He is working in the Middle East.

I hate the news on TV.

There was a bombing in the Middle East. A lot of people were killed. Everyone's watching the same video repeatedly.

Patty's mother broke a tooth from grinding her teeth nervously.

Now Patty thinks her dad is dead, because her mother is so scared.

I asked Patty if she really thought her dad was dead. She said no, she thinks he is smart and that he likely found a place to hide until he could escape. But her mother acts like she knows something.

I told her I think that her dad is probably okay, too. Because we always fear the worst and the news wants us to be afraid. Patty agreed. We both felt better.

I hope her mother calms down.

December 2, 2005

Patty's dad escaped! He is home. I'm not allowed to know anything else.

December 25, 2005

It is Christmas.

I am just going to say this and I don't care what anyone thinks. I am a Catholic. I like my faith. And I am tired of people thinking we're not Christian.

We were the first Christians in the upper room.

Jesus declared Peter the Rock on which our church was built.

OK, it would have been way easier if Jesus said, "Peter, you are going to be the leader of my church and we'll call each person who takes the job after you a Pope."

Anyway, Catholic means universal, so we are the <u>universal</u> Christian church.

Why everything had to get fancy and complicated, I don't know.

The Catholic faith uses a lot of terms like adoration, benediction and transubstantiation.

If I had my way, I'd make sure a definition flashed on the church wall when these terms come up.

The mass and homily would be easier to understand.

Sure, there might be more questions afterward, but isn't that the point? To learn about your faith while also practicing it?

Example: Transubstantiation is when the communion, AKA bread and wine, are blessed to become the body and blood of Christ.

Some might argue, have CSI do an analysis to see if the transformation really happens. Is this the DNA of Jesus?

We know that Jesus said at the Last Supper to do 'this in memory of me'. Communion at mass is our tradition.

I think the bigger question is: why would Jesus want us to eat or drink his body and blood?

It sounds creepy and it would get you put in a mental institution and/or jail if you did this with a real human body!

But the tradition is simply a means of connecting us with the person Jesus, so we understand that God came in the flesh on earth and died, but in rising from the dead we know that we have another life with him.

To know that we will all meet again and have an even better life without pain or worry. That is awesome!

Ok, I need to go to bed.

I should be thinking about this at Easter and not Christmas. Weirdo me.

I'm tired. More later.

BLAIR AT AGE 15

January 8, 2006

Anny died today. No one knows how it happened. She was in her bed and didn't get up for breakfast.

I feel like I want to die!

She didn't look sick or act sick.

I'm not ready for her to die. I mean I knew it would happen someday, but not now!

I went to the facility and they had already stripped her bed.

It looked like someone stole her, bundled her in the sheets and took off.

The mattress was bare. She had an old mattress that she always kept in plastic, but they even took the plastic off.

It looked like new. It was yellow with black pin stripes and buttons. But it seemed naked.

I decided to lay on her bed and see if she was still around —in spirit.

She wasn't.

I really cried then.

Anny's friends came in to talk with me.

They said she went to sleep and never woke up.

I'm not sure how Granny is going to handle this.

I'm not sure how I will.

Her rosary beads were missing.

I looked all over her room and asked the workers where they went.

No one seemed to know.

January 13, 2006

It is Friday the 13th and we had a funeral mass for Anny. There weren't many people there, other than parishioners from our church.

Granny and Anny haven't lived in Florida long enough to make many friends.

We found out that Anny was holding her rosary beads when she died, which doesn't sound like she died in her sleep.

She always prayed in the morning after breakfast, unless she died the day before they discovered her.

I say that because the facility said she died hours before breakfast and she wouldn't be praying the rosary before breakfast.

Mom wants an investigation, but my dad said we need to accept that death happens and Anny probably held her beads for comfort.

Granny feels bad. She moved Anny down here to give her better care and she died too soon.

Granny feels guilty that she has a nice condo on the inter-coastal waterway and new friends.

She thinks God is punishing her selfishness.

I told her if Anny were alive, she'd tell Granny she thinks a lot of herself.

Anny was funny like that. If one of us started to feel guilty, she'd say, 'You think a lot of yourself—that God would take time away from important matters to make you feel guilty. The God of love doesn't make his children feel guilty.'

Anny was smart like that.

She had more faith than all of us put together.

Anny grew up with an abusive mother who beat her regularly.

Anny knew there was something wrong with her mother.

She said God gave her the strength and wisdom to endure her mother's cruelty.

When Anny learned the rosary at ten years old, she prayed every day for her mother to get better.

She said Mary the mother of Jesus became her mother, because someone had to.

Anny never knew her own father and ran away from home at 16.

Her mother never tried to find her.

Anny got a job on a dining car of a train and traveled up and down the east coast.

She said that many of the waiters on the dining cars were older African American men. Anny was a dishwasher. She never explained how she got the job.

The waiters she worked with were protective of her. They only introduced her to young travelers they were familiar with. Young men and women who had manners and said grace before meals.

That is how she met *her Charlie*. My grandpa.

He traveled to trade school by train.

The waiters liked Charlie and asked Anny if she'd like to learn to serve coffee. They gave her a server's coat, and instructed her how. It was the only time she ever served. Women usually worked as maids.

When Anny met grandpa, they immediately fell in love. She said it was a whirlwind courtship and there would never be another man like Charlie.

Anny named my Granny Lana, after Grandpa Charlie's favorite movie star, Lana Turner.

There aren't many pictures of Grandpa Charlie, Anny or Granny when they were young. That makes me sad.

Grandpa Charlie was killed when a car he was working on fell off the lift.

It happened months before Granny was born.

Betty (Anny) and Charlie were only married for two years when he died.

Anny never married again, but raised Granny in the back of the home salon that she opened. It wasn't like now. She didn't have a license to do people's hair. She was good at fixing her own hair. She washed her customer's hair in her kitchen sink and cut and styled at her table. It was the only way she could afford to put food on the table.

I really should stop thinking about the rosary issue.

March 30, 2006

I will have my learner's permit soon and Mo doesn't even want one. It makes me crazy.

Mo likes public transportation. He thinks it is fun to get on a bus and go anywhere in the city with a bunch of other people.

Well, it isn't like we are in a big city. This is just Pinellas County, Florida and the bus goes around to neighborhoods, shopping, downtown, and the beach has a trolley.

We don't go to the beach much, which is because neither of us like sand.

I don't like getting sunburned, either. Mo doesn't get a sunburn, he just gets darker. Plus, Mo likes the indoors. That's another reason he thinks the bus is fun. He can ride and sketch.

I mean, I like the bus, too. But I don't like that you can't tell the bus where to take you, and just go there.

Mo said the adventure is so much more entertaining than just getting to go where you want. He likes all the stops and seeing who gets on.

Mo is going to be a comic book artist/writer. I told him about my diary, just because he sketches out our day anyway, which is like art-journaling. He's a good artist. That's also why we both like going to the children's section of the library. Mo gets inspiration for drawings there.

I guess I'll someday be in my own car and I'll drive beside the bus and watch Mo ride.

That would be seriously funny. It might be dangerous, too. Just because I would be laughing too hard.

April 10, 2006

Mo knows about Michael, and now <u>he</u> wants to meet Gabriel.

He said if he could speak with Gabriel, he would ask him why he showed himself to both Mary, the mother of Jesus and the Prophet Mohammed, Mo's namesake.

I told Mo I didn't think he really wanted to meet Michael or Gabriel; there is too much responsibility that comes with the relationship. Look at me, I'm in therapy with a spiritual adviser, but Mo thinks that's cool.

It's not cool.

That's the curse of being an advocate for angels. See, I am using words like <u>advocate</u>! That's not teen talk.

Example: I was in Confirmation class at church and we were studying about temptation in Luke 4:6-13 and I brought up that while we are all tempted like Jesus was, the real point of the passage was showing how Lucifer fell from grace. He was the brilliant Daystar… and in the Garden he tempted Eve, the same as he tempted Jesus in the desert.

Lucifer was hoping to pull humans down again.

In verse 13 "When the devil had finished every temptation, he departed from him for a time."

But he departed from Jesus not because Jesus stood up for his beliefs, but Jesus the son of God shamed Lucifer for falling from his original position.

SNAP!

And everyone looked at me like I was crazy!

I went on anyway, thinking it would make sense if I explained it right.

I mean, Lucifer had the nerve to say in Luke 4:9 "He (God) will command his angels concerning you, to guard you, and: With their hands they will support you, lest you dash your foot against a stone."

This is a fallen angel saying this!

Lucifer is talking to God (through Jesus), and Jesus says (as God would to his fallen angel), "You shall not put the Lord, your God, to the test."

POW!

Because the fallen angel/devil did that in the Garden of Eden.

Temptation isn't so much about being duped, it's also about being a tempter, which Eve became.

It isn't about sinning; it's about being an agent of sin.

The angels are guardians and helpers for God and protectors. But Lucifer's statement to Jesus was tricky. He was trying to say the angels would be there for Jesus if he joined Lucifer, but it wouldn't be the good angels, it would be the fallen angels! The demons!

When Lucifer fell, he became an agent of sin and that is what hell was created for, the agents of sin and sinners who don't repent.

Anyway, it is far easier to seek forgiveness than to change a habit of deceiving others, because your reality is distorted and you really believe that what was wrong is right, like greed… If you make money doing something illegal and give money to help someone, you feel your money helps, and therefore the way you gained it isn't so bad.

And after all that, Mrs. Cartwright, my Confirmation teacher said, "And what saint name have you chosen?"

She totally dismissed everything.

Why do adults do that? Was she listening at all?

April 18, 2006

Mo and I were sitting in Father Murphy's waiting area today. I figured Mo may as well talk to a priest, since he is fixated on what I'm going through.

I said I'd go with him to his mosque. He said he didn't need to teach me the faith he was raised in. He is looking for enlightenment from many sources. He wants to learn and make his own decisions.

Mo also said that I am firm in my faith. He is looking for that strength within.

He said I have a knowing.

I'm not trying to convert him. I am just honoring his wish to learn and see what he thinks.

Mo's parents are super nice and we all get along. But it is not like our families hang out together. In fact, my family and his family are similar, we all just hang out with our own families, except when there is a party or event at school that brings everyone together.

I don't know if that is good or bad. It isn't like anyone is avoiding each other. It is like life is a routine of school, work, eating, sleeping and weekends.

Gosh, that seems really boring now that I think about it.

Anyway, Bishop Wright was in Father Murphy's office. The bishop had his entourage with him and I'm still not sure if Father Murphy is in trouble... or getting an award.

The bishop has a couple of assistants. One drove him and I'm not sure what the other one does. They are like the Diocesan Secret Service. Well, that isn't true, but that is what it looked like to us.

Mo was so impressed.

We just sat there in the church office surveying the religious paintings and saintly art.

We did some homework while we were waiting. Everything was super quiet. We really didn't feel comfortable talking, because we get loud when we start laughing and cracking on each other.

Since the church is only a few blocks from my house, we just decided to stop in on our way home from school.

Anyway, Mo asked why some priests and their assistants are so heavy (he said fat) when they made a vow of poverty.

I wasn't sure, but I told Mo that I know they eat at parishioner's homes. Especially at the older people's homes. I think it is because the church wants to be remembered in the old people's wills, so the priests make themselves available for dinner.

Anyway, my neighbor said the Catholic church is wealthy and by the size of some priests, that is a lot of home cooked dinners. I'm just guessing.

The bishop mentioned in his homily once that he received too many fruitcakes one Christmas, so it all makes sense.

He also told us he was originally from New England and raised by a single mother. (That has nothing to do with his weight). But anyway, he said he never knew his father, who was lost at sea during a major storm when he was a boy.

The bishop said he felt his priestly calling after he heard that Jesus' disciples were fishermen. He figured his dad was away helping Jesus.

When Bishop Wright finally came out of Father Murphy's office he pointed at me and said, "there she is."

He looked right at me.

Mo stared at me, like he was seeing me for the first time.

I said nothing.

"We've heard about the miracle storm," he said.

"Sorry." I was embarrassed.

"Are you?" He asked.

"No, Father. But I figured that is what adults want kids to say."

Then Father Murphy wanted to be a part of the conversation. "Blair's spiritual advisor is Sister Jo."

Bishop Wright smiled and nodded. He then reached out his hand toward Mo.

"Who is your friend, Blair?" Bishop Wright asked.

Before I could say anything, Mo answered, "I'm Mo."

Mo stood and shook the bishop's hand.

The bishop gave Mo a firm handshake.

"You're in good company, Mo," Bishop Wright said. Then he pats us both on the head.

That was lame!

His assistants appeared out of nowhere.

Literally.

Mo was speechless. He didn't get a chance to talk with Father Murphy, who was called away to see a dying parishioner. The bishop and Father Murphy left at the same time.

Mo and I went into the main church and spent some time in there.

While I was praying, Mo seemed to be thinking, but I didn't ask him about what. Because every so often, I would glance at him and he would be either grinning or frowning.

I'm just sorry he didn't get more out of the day.

That's another thing that bothers me about adults. They are always telling kids that they will make time to talk or answer questions and they never do.

I mean why does the church talk about vocations to religious life, the lack of priests and then just run off? For all they know, Mo could possibly be the next pope.

Not that Father Murphy shouldn't see a dying parishioner... but maybe he should have invited us to go with him?

That would have been a cool gesture—at least we'd feel like he was interested.

I wonder what a dying person would think of two teens joining a priest on his rounds?

May 3, 2006

I am praying for our scripture study group. They were sooo negative tonight. Everyone was dwelling on the international news and all the bad things that are happening in the world.

Then, they got into a discussion that hell is on earth and they can't wait to get to heaven. The whole Adam and Eve thing.

I recited Genesis 1:31 to them.

God saw all that he had made, and it was very good.

God didn't make an evil world and just because people sin doesn't make the world an evil place. The animals, the trees and oceans and plants aren't evil.

Well, that unleashed a whole mess of "you're too young to understand..."

I just excused myself to go to the restroom and walked home. I doubt they even knew I was gone.

May 21, 2006

Sister Jo asked me to join her at a healing mass so I could have a mission priest pray over me.

She didn't think I was sick or needed to be healed, but wanted me to receive a blessing.

The mission calls it a healing.

I'm not sure why, but I guess some people need to feel healed from what troubles them and some really need healing from illnesses.

Sister Jo didn't think I was troubled, either. It was more like a spiritual immunization or antidote to possible darkness that could attack me.

She said I might pass out, but it would be okay.

She said that many people pass out, which is called Slain in the Spirit. This is a real Catholic thing.

Glad my mother isn't going with us, because she'd probably be way too fascinated by this and only want to go to charismatic masses.

It isn't a charismatic mass though, but a healing service. It is something that people in the charismatic movement do, these healing services. Which is not the same as a blessing of the sick or last rites—which is standard Catholic stuff.

Anyway, I know of charismatics because one Saturday night I was riding my bike and saw that our church parking lot was full. It wasn't a normal mass time, so I went in.

I thought it might be a wedding and I wanted to check it out and have some cake if they were using the reception hall, but it was a charismatic mass.

I didn't like the charismatics.

It was like regular Catholics on pills. It just seemed too hippie-like.

Their masses seem like Protestant tent revivals to me. But there are no snakes, at least I didn't see any.

I'm no super Catholic, but it sure seems like we would have snakes, given the whole serpent in the Garden of Eden.

I know we don't have snakes because Grandma Iris told me that we are civilized and don't practice the way the 'holy rollers' do. Holy rollers speak in tongues, roll around on the floor and handle snakes.

Grandma Iris would not approve of the charismatics. They do speak in tongues if the spirit moves them and they don't sit still.

I guess Grandma Iris isn't the expert I thought she was, since there are uncivilized Catholics, as she would call them.

Anyway, a charismatic mass is all touchy-feely, swaying and crying out.

Grandma Iris would never go to a charismatic mass. She's the more sophisticated Catholic of our family.

When Sister Jo asked me to go to the healing service, I didn't tell Grandma Iris, but agreed out of respect for Sr. Jo.

I keep an open mind.

May 22, 2006

Ok, I went to the healing service yesterday.

The priest gave a talk before the healing part began.

The church was full. I mean, like Christmas. He said everyone there was called to be there.

That blew my mind.

He said we were all in this one place because we were supposed to be there. God ordained it, so to speak.

I looked around at the different people. There were all ages and races. It was like I imagined the first Pentecost to be. Every nationality represented and even if we spoke different languages, we'd all be able to understand each other.

Sister and I didn't go for the healing right away. We sat watching others.

I couldn't figure out why some people got a nudge on the forehead and others didn't.

Those who got the nudge went straight to the floor. These were the people who are Slain in the Spirit.

The church had catchers who gently placed the Slain on the floor, until they woke.

I wanted to laugh, because I just imagined one of the catchers being off their game and oops, someone really falls. Of course, that would be terrible, but my mind works like that.

When it was our turn, I got the nudge, but I wasn't going down. I was not going to do that. I think I just imagined disappointing my Grandma Iris and wasn't in the moment. The priest told a Comforter to hug me.

The lady's badge read: Comforter. Which caught me off guard, because I didn't see those people from where we were sitting.

When the Comforter hugged me, I just cried like a baby. Sister Jo also got a hug, but she was totally cool about it.

I was so upset. I couldn't understand why I was crying. It was like the time I had my wisdom teeth pulled and I was coming out of sedation and cried constantly. But that was a drug reaction.

This was so internal that I know Jo will want to talk with me about it at some point.

I was a total embarrassment.

It was like a crying bomb went off inside of me and I just couldn't turn it off. I guess I should have just gone to the floor when I got the nudge, but no, I had to fight it and become the crier of all criers!

I was wondering if the Comforter was someone special. I didn't know the lady, but wow, I guess I really needed a hug.

Or maybe, because I don't cry much, I just let out a load at one time?

Some people wailed all kinds of sad things and spoke in tongues. I wasn't certain about those people.

They were extremely tormented. But seemed healed when they came out of it.

I received a spiritual rider, too. It is a term I made up.

Sister Jo does not believe in what I am sharing. But I am very certain that Saint Paul through the intercession of the Holy Spirit stayed close guard with me.

It was as though the crying opened me up to receive something. I felt like Paul possessed me.

Possession is something demons do, not saints.

But I don't know what else to call it. It was like someone was holding me from the inside. Like an internal hug.

It was a wonderful feeling. It was like an electricity from my core and my vision was all fuzzy and then clear.

Why Paul?

I can't explain it, but Paul was blinded when he was Saul on the road to Damascus because he was persecuting Christians. Jesus gave him his sight back after three days and he became Paul, the best witness to the faith after the 12 apostles. Some think early Christianity would have lost its appeal without someone like Paul to keep the faith going.

I am not someone who persecutes like Saul did, but I feel certain that it was Paul.

I believe Paul, like Michael, supports the call God has in my mission on earth. Paul was instrumental in the continuation of the faith.

The future is <u>faithless</u>.

Only Paul could understand what the persecutors of the future have in store for the world. If Michael and Sister Jo feel I need to write my visions, then Paul would have to be the one holding me.

I know this isn't going to make sense to anyone, but I know what I <u>know</u>.

It was Paul. He is my Obi-Wan Kenobi mentor and I'm his Luke Skywalker.

May 24, 2006

Paul left.

It was like I was carried for three days, so that I would receive a gift.

An insight. Now to figure it out.

May 30, 2006

My dad is teaching me to change the oil in our family car.

He totally forgot to put the plug thing in before I started pouring the new oil in and we couldn't stop laughing.

I almost peed my pants.

I really like being with my dad because nothing sad, weird or mysterious happens when we are hanging out. He is my comic relief.

June 16, 2006

Mo and I went to the beer-can building in downtown Tampa today.

We took the bus. Mo's cousin, Sam (that's what he calls himself in the American language) is a security guard there.

It is a bank building that is called the beer-can building because it is totally round. But it is nowhere near Busch Gardens which is named for beer.

Funny, Busch Gardens should totally own the beer-can building.

We love the view from the top. It has a great view of the University of Tampa.

The university architecture looks like an enchanted kingdom with these silver pointy bedposts mounted on the buildings. I don't know what they call that, but it is medieval or looks like what I think Camelot might be like.

Anyway, we think the campus looks better from the beer-can.

Mo and I want to attend college in a metropolitan city and go to museums and theater and really enjoy culture.

We think Tampa has so much potential, but it's boring. There's nothing for us to do.

We sat and just watched the city. We barely said a word.

Mo stared at the skyline a lot!

Beauty depresses him. I could feel it. I had to hide my face and just punch him in the shoulder as I didn't want him to see my tears, which mirrored his.

I hate feeling people's pain. I can't control their emotions, yet sometimes I experience a lot of their thoughts and physical sensations. It's creepy.

Mo asked me if God would help him talk to his parents. And I said, "Of course, but you may have to tell them Allah spoke to you. That's what they believe in."

He didn't laugh when I punched him this time. He just walked away, so I knew it was bad. I said a prayer right then.

I had to shake his thoughts.

"Hey Mo, I want to get a smoothie on our way home." He just nodded like whatever.

We took the bus to south Howard Avenue and found a cool natural food store that had a wooden statue of Gabriel outside! Like a wooden Indian, but a wooden angel. Gabe's Whole Food Emporium.

Mo figured it was God speaking to him so he perked up a bit.

We went in and just browsed all the books and Mo read a paper about how health foods help you think better. He liked that.

June 26, 2006

I got a job! I'm filing for a dentist's office a few blocks from our house. I only work a few hours a couple of days a week. Dr. Bartlett is a forensic dentist and he doesn't see many patients. He is mostly an expert witness to identify people who are missing or dead.

He is very unorganized!

He has x-rays and papers stacked all over his office.

Well, those are the cases he is working on. He said it is an <u>organized</u> clutter, and he knows where everything is.

I'm concerned that he won't find anything once we really get things in order. Some of the films and papers don't fit well into regular folders, so I recommended we get some plastic containers that fit odd shapes.

He loved the idea.

We're even making regular files that say where the oddball files are stored. We're also labeling the containers numerically so they'll be easy to retrieve.

I'm going to open a savings account once I have $100. I think I'm going to save up for a nice camera.

I want to start photographing things and nature.

September 9, 2006

Someday somebody's gonna read this and think I'm crazy. I just don't know how to say this any clearer, I saw demons today. Hundreds of them swarming like gnats and they were not small.

I'm guessing the Holy Spirit has hold of my brain, because I'm not wigged out or scared. Otherwise, I should be scared to death! Right?

The demons were the size of a medium cat and gross! Gray flesh with big heads and saw-blade teeth, and they were attacking Sister Jo.

One possessed her for a few minutes and Michael pulled it out of her. I saw it!

God sent me to the church to keep Father Murphy from exiting at that time. Thank goodness Michael was there to save Sister Jo. I just don't understand how God decides who will get protection from an archangel and who just fends for themselves?

I also overheard my parents arguing recently about who I am more like; like they are jealous. Believe me, they wouldn't have wanted to be me today! My mother would have had a heart attack and my father would have been stupid enough to think he could help Michael fight.

The fact that I see St. Michael the Archangel is crazy enough, but to witness Satan's helpers! I don't know how I am going to grow up normal now.

Who do I talk to? Other than Sister Jo? Father Murphy doesn't know how to handle anything supernatural, in fact, he's totally blind to it!

How does God show a dumb kid all of this and his devoted priest can't see a thing? Of course, I already know the answer. He's not ready.

Like I am? What makes me ready?

My Mom keeps talking on the phone to one of her co-workers who is very depressed, I hate to break the news to her, but I don't think her friend is going to survive.

Mom spends hours talking this woman and I know it's good for her to help people. But it isn't going to change the outcome.

Well, I've got to do some homework.

Sept 10, 2006

I had a nightmare after seeing the demons yesterday. In my dream, they were trying to recruit me.

I escaped into a house that had many rooms and the rooms were all different. Most of the rooms I remember were organized and then I found one that looked like a chapel, but I got locked in one that was full of cobwebs.

The cobwebs were thick and tangled around me and I couldn't find my way out. Then the door disappeared.

There were windows when I entered, but I couldn't see the windows later as the cobwebs entangled me like a net.

I struggled under a light bulb that was dangling from a cord above me.

And the webs got stuck to the bulb and started burning. Then the bulb exploded and I woke up.

I was flailing in my sleep, afraid that I had glass in my eyes.

I told Mo my dream today and he said the coolest thing.

He said the light bulb might be the ideas the demons wanted to plant in my mind, but they weren't allowed in, so they exploded.

Sept 11, 2006

I had a session with Sister Jo this afternoon, we didn't discuss what I saw. I don't think she even knows that a demon possessed her. I wanted to say something but held my tongue.

Today is the fifth anniversary of 9/11 and it almost seems that people are getting used to it being a terrible event in the past, like Pearl Harbor. Anny was alive back then and said Pearl Harbor felt like the world was ending.

Sr. Jo seems different. She said her vision is off. She asked if we could just close our eyes and meditate.

I didn't stay long.

I'm really worried for her and now I wish Michael would show up! I have questions for him.

September 14, 2006

I had a God-flash today. I was holding Anny's bible and I started shaking. I shut my eyes and the next thing I knew I was holding a different book and standing on a window ledge. I started to fall and woke on the floor of my bedroom.

I woke as I was falling. Anny's bible was on the floor and I turned it over and read parts of Jeremiah 31: 7-8.

> "Save, O LORD, your people,
> the remnant of Israel."
> See, I am going to bring them from the land of the north,
> and gather them from the farthest parts of the earth

I don't really know what this means, but it seems like I should understand it. Like somehow, somewhere in time, this passage will make sense to the people in my visions.

The God-flash felt real. More so than any I have ever had.

What if this is like Sr. Jo's possession? I wonder if someone else saw me?

Is there something I should know? I looked at the calendar. Today is September 14th.

Why today?

Something is coming. I know something is coming. Why does this seem or feel separate or apart from the vision?

I started crying and didn't feel I could stop.

Then I remembered the healing service. This crying felt similar.

Am I losing my mind? Is that what this is all about?

Am I crazy?

Did I really see Jo get possessed by a demon?

I wonder if the ledge I saw in the God-flash is where my insanity takes me?

I hugged Anny's bible and remembered what Anny told me about Saint Faustina. That Faustina was given the Divine Mercy prayer because of her great faith.

But I don't have great faith, I'm crazy!

No one sees or understands what I do and now Sister Jo is sick.

That's it!!

That is why the demons attacked Sr. Jo!

To keep Jo from helping me help Sybille.

Once I calmed down, I decided to do an online search and discovered Sept. 14, is the day Faustina received the Divine Mercy Chaplet (prayer). It was over the dates of Sept 13 to the 14th 1935.

My Anny was alive in 1935 and today is SEPTEMBER 14th!

Maybe Anny is trying to help me understand?

September 30, 2006

I am feeling better about Sister Jo.

She has tinted glasses that are helping her to see better. She said the light isn't as harsh that way.

I joked with her that she better not become too light-sensitive, because she wants to be able to go into the light when her time comes.

We both laughed.

But it got me thinking...

How does a person become light-sensitive? Or is it only evil that makes us light-sensitive?

What infects us inside that causes the light to dim?

I better stop thinking about this. I don't need to invite the *light-sensitive* for a discussion.

I'm going to pray the Our Father and then I need to go to the mall for some science fair materials.

October 11, 2006

I am so bored. I wanted to ride my bike, but the tire was flat.

Then I tried to change the tube like my Dad taught me, but I didn't do something right. It frustrated me.

My mom and dad weren't home, so I went for a walk.

Walking is boring. My neighborhood isn't very exciting. The sidewalks are all cracked and lifting like there is something trying to escape below the concrete.

It is the tree roots pushing up the concrete, but I can't believe tree roots can break concrete!

I can't break concrete.

Karate people can break concrete with their bare hands, but I'd have to jump on it or use a hammer.

How is it that thin tree roots have a way of breaking through the earth and saying, "concrete, you are not welcome."

Snap!

If I had been on my bike, I wouldn't have noticed the sidewalks as much.

I wish we had a store nearby. I want candy. I could get candy on my bike, because I can go farther.

I am not walking all the way to the convenience store. It is like 3 miles away.

I did see a smashed dead mouse on the road, though. I'm beginning to wonder about the mice in our area. It was so flat that I wonder how long it took to dry like that.

Where are the vultures?

I thought vultures seek dead animals and eat them. Isn't that the circle of life? The survival of the fittest?

Maybe the mouse died after being attacked by a cat and then got run over by a car?

If a car smashes a mouse, does it disrupt the vulture's sense of death? Because a smashed body is not easy to smell or pick apart?

I guess nature can disrupt the material world like the tree roots breaking the sidewalk.

Okay, I was wrong, walking is interesting.

October 13, 2006

Today is Friday the 13th, so my Mom and I went antiquing today. It is her thing. She likes to collect hand mirrors and vanity sets. Powder puffs, combs, etc.

I spotted a set on a buffet and started toward it and had the worst force hit me. I was stopped! I couldn't go any further. Seriously. It was like someone threw an invisible net over me and just nailed it to the floor and I couldn't move forward.

I could turn around and go backward, but I couldn't move forward.

Then she appeared. It was a beautiful woman who just stared at me.

She had her hair pulled up in that poufy style from the 1800s and she wore a white dress that went to the floor. It wasn't a wedding dress. It just looked like a nice dress.

She wasn't mean or happy. She just blocked me from going toward that vanity set.

There were other people in the store.

But no one seemed to notice that I was just standing there like a freak. Not moving.

I backed up.

Then I rushed to the section where my mother was.

I had the dumbest conversation with her.

I said, "You do realize these things belonged to other people before?"

She cracked up and said, "They are antiques, Blair. That means they are old and yes, someone enjoyed them a long time ago."

"Or they didn't enjoy them?" I said.

Mom just looked at me oddly and said, "You have a point."

Then she asked if I was all right. She said I looked pale.

I looked back to where the lady ghost was. She was fixed. Watching me. She didn't smile or frown.

I told my mother we needed to leave. That a ghost in the front of the store didn't want anyone touching her stuff.

Mom said, "How did her stuff get here if she doesn't want her stuff touched? Someone had to bring it here."

I thought about it and realized this ghost didn't want ME touching her stuff.

"She must have..." I said, then whispered "been unpacked with her stuff."

Mom got really wigged out by that.

That seemed to draw the lady ghost to us. She was standing by my mother. Mom must have felt her presence. Mom froze.

I grabbed my mother's hand and walked swiftly through the maze of stuff and out of the store.

Mom seemed to understand and kept pace with me. When we were outside, the ghost just watched from the window.

We didn't talk about it ever, not in the car, at home or anytime.

Mom came home and boxed up everything in her antique collection and donated them to a local thrift shop and vowed to never antique again. She said she was too afraid to throw the items away and hoped nothing was attached to the pieces she had.

I get shivers just thinking about the elegant ghost. I wanted to pray the moment I saw her, but it felt like she paralyzed that part of my thinking.

I guess the lady ghost avoided going into the light because that meant parting with her stuff.

Well they say you can't take it with you. But no one ever said you could stay with it, either.

October 18, 2006

Dr. Bartlett got the weirdest case today.

He got replicas of a type of dog mouth that mauled someone to death.

He doesn't take animal forensics cases, but he agreed to this one.

Dr. Bartlett said it didn't represent any animal he or the veterinary forensic specialists had ever seen. He said the doctor who had the case before him died of a heart attack before he could document his findings.

That worried me.

I don't think it is an animal.

October 26, 2006

Michael showed up today. I was in Driver's Education and he stood in the back of the room listening.

It wasn't my day to drive, so I'm not sure why he needed to attend the class. Not like I was in danger of running anyone down.

Anyway, I started doodling and Michael came over and whispered, "Pay attention."

My teacher looked at me oddly. I was wondering if he could see Michael. It was like Michael was prompting him.

The teacher said, "Blair, can you explain what to do when you are approaching a yellow light?"

I said, "Well my Mom doesn't do anything different, but it means yield."

Michael then waved over my guardian angel. It was my first time seeing her. She materialized at a wave of his hand and said, "I'm watching over you", and she stepped back and faded out. It was like a split second.

It was so weird. It was like my guardian angel was just appeasing Michael and taking off.

Michael didn't even introduce us.

I understand that he wants me to be safe. But seriously, isn't life preordained? I mean, my Mom says everything happens for a reason.

I am sure that means even if I am a bad driver, an accident doesn't necessarily mean the end.

Unless that is meant to be. Right?

Michael left once I stopped doodling.

October 27, 2006

Michael decided to make a point and rode in the backseat of the Driver's Ed car today.

Who else gets Michael the Archangel as a backseat driver?

I mean seriously, it must be his day off or something?

I was looking in the rear-view mirror making faces at him and my instructor gave me points off.

My teacher thought I was mocking <u>him</u> when I was really rolling my eyes at Michael.

Michael said, "This is where your friends will be riding. You shouldn't pay so much attention to your passengers. This is a machine and you are the operator."

I laughed at Michael saying a car was a "machine" and got an F. Right!

Like I'm going to tell my teacher that Michael was distracting me?

Okay, I get his point.

Michael doesn't want me to let my friends divert my attention from the road.

October 28, 2006

I'm grounded. My Driver's Ed teacher called my parents and said I'm disrespectful. I may have to retake the class.

Mom knows how I can think of something funny and start randomly laughing, so she figured that was what happened.

I just nodded.

I hope that's not considered lying.

Oh crap!

It is lying.

Well, I guess I need to go to confession.

October 29, 2006

Since I'm grounded and I'm altar serving this weekend, I figured I may as well go to 2 p.m. confession.

So I walked over to the church. I was scheduled to altar serve the 4 p.m. mass—so I figured I'd just hang out and help if needed.

I go into the confessional and our visiting priest Father McCarthy is in the confessional.

He is older and super funny.

FYI—There is an option to sit across from the priest and there is an option to kneel behind the screen.

I usually sit and face the priest, but this time I decided to kneel behind the screen.

I really felt guilty for lying to my mom.

I said, "Bless me father for I have sinned, it has been two months since my last confession."

Father McCarthy said, "Yes, Blair."

Then I felt stupid!

I mean priests don't address you by name in confession, but I felt this was my chance to come clean. Father McCarthy is so easy going and there was no need to hide.

I moved to the seat and faced Father McCarthy.

"I've lied. I've been ignoring my responsibilities. I've been disrespectful to my parents and elders. Plus, I'm envious of my friends, because I don't know why God wants more from me than them? I'm not really sure what God wants me to do."

Since Father McCarthy knows I see Sister Jo for spiritual direction, he focused on the sins of lying, disrespect and envy. He did say that my work with Sister Jo will help me with the direction God wants me to take.

But for my penance, he gave me some Our Fathers and Hail Marys and for one month to watch what happens daily to a tree or plant in our yard.

See what happens to it. Does it grow, does it shed leaves, does it wilt? Did it rain during that time? Was it sunny? What happens?

He said this would help me understand how God works.

He said that I shouldn't tell anyone I am doing this, because I need to see the changes as God does.

I am only to watch.

I decided I'm going to watch a palm tree in our backyard. We have several and they are all different, but there is one in the corner of the yard and I can just look out the sliding glass door and see it.

He said I'm only to watch, but I'm going to make notes.

My first note was that the palm tree has pods that look like thick, cylinder husks with hard pointy tips. It looks like all the fronds are healthy, except one is turning brown. The tree is probably ten feet tall and there are rocks around the base.

This penance makes me feel productive.

Like forgiveness is about understanding vs. feeling guilty.

October 30, 2006

Michael is becoming a frequent visitor.

I caught him watching television with my parents!

I walked in and Michael was unaware of my presence, or so I thought.

Then Michael turned and started talking to me about the news at the same time my dad was also talking to my mother about the news. It was really confusing.

The news reported an outbreak of a deadly virus in Africa and they said it was germ warfare.

Michael said that it was difficult to battle demons that infect people.

I said, "I didn't know viruses were demonic."

My parents stopped and looked at me.

My Dad said, "Did you say demonic virus?"

I looked at Michael, like, *help me out.*

He didn't. They all three looked at me.

"I'm going to my room," I said and just walked out.

Michael is going to get an earful next time we talk.

Also, one pod on the palm burst open and there are bees buzzing around the flowers in the pod.

October 31, 2006 All Souls Day

I am dressing up for Halloween as St. Joan of Arc. It is a good way to celebrate two holidays in one. Today is All Souls Day, which is a remembrance of people who passed away. I will be thinking about my Anny.

Tomorrow is All Saints Day, which is a remembrance of all the Saints who are in heaven.

Halloween is a lot of fun. A lot of businesses let their employees dress in costume.

Mo is dressing as Bart Simpson. Mo wanted me to dress as Marge or Lisa Simpson and I said I'd rather be Maggie Simpson.

We worked on our costumes last night. I have a cardboard plate of armor that I painted and I have brown tights, a tan shirt and skort. My shield and sword are also cardboard. I painted them in shades of silver and bronze.

We both bought wigs at the party store. Mine is just short brown hair. Mo made his yellow wig spiky like Bart's hair. He also got whiffle balls and my dad cut them in half so Mo could have a pair of eyes.

Mo tied the eyes to a string that wraps around his ears and a piece that connects over his nose.

It was so funny looking! I can't wait to see him at school.

Mo is finally hanging out with more guys at school. He doesn't rely on me as much.

I've got other friends, too.

But I think our geek days are ending.

We will always be geeks, but it seems we have less in common.

Mo now watches sports on TV regularly and he's really into it. He is also talking about becoming a pharmacist or veterinarian, instead of a comic book artist.

I'm still undecided what I want to do. Okay, I've got to get ready for school.

November 1, 2006 All Saints Day

Yesterday was fun, but I got into a mock sword fight with a student dressed as Harry Potter.

Harry's sword was made of wood. He crushed my cardboard sword, which is okay. But what wasn't okay, was he jabbed me with his sword and gave me a bruise in the gut.

I laughed it off, but it hurt.

This guy's kind of a bully, because he didn't say he was sorry.

Mo wasn't there for the sword fight. He stuck with his guy friends and we didn't really talk until it was time to go home.

When I told him about the bruise he said, well Joan went to battle right? What are you complaining about? Don't you girls want equal status?

I punched Mo in the arm.

I told him that I was not Joan—and not in a real battle with Harry Potter and that no one has a reason to hurt me!

We were celebrating Halloween. How does that equal me deserving to get a wooden sword to the stomach?

Mo punched me back. Harder than I hit him.

He said I wasn't allowed to punch him if he wasn't allowed to punch me.

I really wanted to cry, but I didn't.

Mo's right.

Dang he punched me hard!

I have been wrong in punching him, but he still didn't care about Harry Potter hurting me?!

I felt like Mo's punch was something he had planned for this moment. Like all the times I've punched him added up to this. I think I am going to have two bruises now.

Anyway, my parents, Granny and I are going to mass tonight.

All Saints Day is a Holy Day of obligation. Meaning we should go, we're obligated.

Well, that's what Granny says.

These masses are always shorter.

I wish we were more like Protestants in some ways, they do fellowship and potlucks more often than Catholics.

We're Sunday coffee-and-donuts/fish fry for Lent kind of worshipers.

I think that is why these other Christian faiths have gained such popularity.

I mean, I really like potluck dinners!

My mom makes the same thing for dinner every week.

She would never make a broccoli salad or a pineapple upside down cake, much less a ham salad with cheddar cheese and green peas.

When we get invited to a potluck, mom buys something to take, like wings, or she makes spaghetti.

Boring!

I hope I don't fall asleep at church.

Funny, Michael never shows up for mass. What's that about?

November 8, 2006

I totally forgot to check the palm for several days and I finally went out and my dad was trimming it. He cut away the pods and the wilted flowers and a dangling frond that was still attached.

I'm trying to remember the point of this project? I guess I'm learning how we humans don't keep up with how fast things change.

I guess my dad does, because he trims the palms.

Huh...

My dad tends to the yard and he knows what is happening to the plants and the grass. He takes responsibility for these things.

I never realized how much he does, because the yard always looks good.

Well, I'm not sure I'm going to remember to complete this project of watching the palm because I have a lot going on.

Is that the point? That we humans aren't patient enough to see God's glory daily?

November 10, 2006

I am staying with my Grandma Iris this weekend!

We always go to the best places for lunch and we usually go to a theater production.

Grandma supports professional theater in Orlando. That means she gets season tickets.

My Grandpa Bill died before I was born, he and Grandma Iris went to shows together when they were dating. My dad said he liked to go to plays with his parents when he was little.

Grandma has several friends who rotate going with her throughout the season since she lives alone.

The restaurants she takes me to for lunch are really sophisticated. White tablecloths and fancy silverware. Grandma has good taste.

Anyway, on Saturdays we go to her church early in the morning and clean. She is a member of the Altar Society.

We vacuum, polish and fill the Holy Water container with water the priest blesses.

We also put out the flowers for mass.

It is all done quietly.

The women who do this have a ritual of being quiet and respectful. They all know what they are doing.

Grandma's church has a lot of old ornate statues and stained-glass windows. It feels ancient.

However, their saint statues are creepy. They have glass eyes that make you feel like they are watching you.

My dad said that when he was little, he used to sit in the church and color when his mother was cleaning. The statues creeped him out, too.

He didn't like being alone with them.

Funny how a Jesus statue can make you uneasy.

I now understand people who are afraid of clowns.

Clowns are supposed to be funny, but the makeup makes you apprehensive.

Anyway, Grandma wants to take me to New York City soon so we can see a Broadway show. I have always wanted to see Times Square and I can't wait to tell Mom.

November 15, 2006

I was considering Alexandrina (da Costa) for my Confirmation name, but I'm worried she might try to convert me to fasting.

I love food and I am not looking to sacrifice that. I know that sounds bad and not committed to my faith, but saints are super devout and kind of crazy.

The saints would agree with me.

I want a saint that I can identify with. That is the point of picking a name.

Alexandrina fasted from all food for I think 13 years and only received daily communion. She was paralyzed and well, maybe only eating one meal a day had something to do with it?

I think I'm going with St. Clare.

I know Clare sounds a lot like Blair, but Clare is the patron saint of television. It is said that she saw visions of the mass on a wall in her room when she was too sick to attend.

Clare scared off an army by just holding up the Blessed Sacrament (which is the consecrated bread and wine used at mass).

She sounds pretty cool and I'm thinking if she shows up, we'll just watch some TV.

Plus, Clare was friends with St. Francis and they are both from Assisi. She took care of him in his old age and Francis is like a top saint.

Everyone knows Francis by his prayer for peace and love of animals.

What a combo: television, animals, peace and scaring bad people with bread and wine. Sign me up!

December 30, 2006

I've had the best month ever. Nothing weird happened. No God-flashes, no Michael, no bad dreams, no worries.

Plus, I got all As on my tests at school.

I'm now in two sports, basketball and swimming.

I'm also thinking of trying photography. And Mo told me that someone has a crush on me.

I feel great!

But I'm also feeling guilty, too.

I haven't started writing the vision for Sybille.

I guess this is what Michael meant, that he didn't want me to get lazy and not help save the future.

That sounds ridiculous!

Me, an instrument in saving the future.

However, I think that is the way the devil works. Causing doubt.

Or helping us to keep too busy.

BLAIR AT AGE 16

January 1, 2007

Happy New Year world!

My mother is resolving to lose weight again and my dad said he'll try to read more. I'm not sure what I'm going to do.

I'd like to take a painting class. I could paint the palm tree. That would be cool.

Or I'd like to win a trophy for basketball.

January 12, 2007

Sister Jo had a lot going on today.

She was so tired. She is also my confirmation sponsor.

Anyway, she does hospital visits and gives communion to shut-ins, so we didn't take the time we normally do to talk.

But one thing we did discuss was my reluctance to write the vision. I don't know why I have been stubborn about this.

I was thinking about Moses and how God made the Pharaoh stubborn.

Is God making me stubborn?

Or is it just my own unwillingness?

I guess free will is making me lazy.

I'm not ready.

Not yet.

February 8, 2007

I just realized that all the TV news about Baghdad is about an ancient biblical city.

Why don't we talk about it in this context?

I need to understand how this all relates the visions I have. What is the bible prophesy?

I guess I need to speak with Michael about this.

Maybe this is why I haven't written the vision.

I'm so busy with school that I can't process all of this.

Hopefully, the internet will be a good resource.

I suppose I could talk with Sr. Jo or Father Murphy, but I really want to figure this out myself.

Do a little detective work.

February 16, 2007

I tried to research Baghdad and I learned that Babylon was the biblical region.

I'm confused.

The Old Testament is so hard to understand at times. I can't figure out the prophesy.

The internet isn't helping.

I want to understand why each religion has a set of rules that points the finger at someone else's faith as being wrong.

God said there will be no other gods before him, but seriously, how can armies of people kill in the name of their beliefs?

I'm clueless.

It isn't like fighting demons.

Demons are so gross.

Wait!

I just realized, if Michael hadn't pulled the demon out of Sister Jo, she may have become one.

Oh.

But I can't feel sorry for the demons, because I don't know their origin. See, that is tricky, too.

Demons who infect humans are the ones who confuse everyone into believing in war, fighting and territorial battles.

Right?

In the book of Matthew, it says a good tree cannot bear bad fruit and bad tree cannot bear good fruit.

The serpent in the garden of good and evil was like an infomercial host that sells us on getting skinny.

Eve knew not to eat it, but bought into the serpent's pitch.

Humans are so easily sold.

I'm not going to try and figure out the bible prophesy of the middle east, or war, or anything that will try to divert me from loving others.

Hey, that _is_ the point!!

We have too much information at our fingertips and we can spin it to whatever we think... so our opinion is right.

No one wants to be wrong.

That hurts their pride.

And we all know that pride is not a virtue.

That is the hard part of being human.

Simple things are just not that exciting.

We want to use our intellect to read between the lines.

But there are no lines between good and evil. It is one or the other.

I think that is why God made an example of children.

If we have the faith of a little kid, we would trust, enjoy and love others.

Kids become afraid, bratty and mean when they are treated unkind or spoiled.

People need to get back to basics!

I'm not going to dwell on the middle east.

April 8, 2007

Well after all the months of prep, I got Confirmed today.

I'm an official Soldier for Christ.

Sealed with the Holy Spirit.

I got emotional when we sang the Litany of Saints hymn.

That is the song where we say the name of each saint, followed by "Pray for Us."

I can't seem to hold it together when that hymn is sung.

I looked when St. Michael, St. Gabriel, St. Raphael were called. Michael didn't show up. I really hoped he would.

He is the ultimate soldier for Christ.

Sister Jo looked weak today.

I think she is still spiritually strong, but that demon did something to her.

She gave me a wooden cross on a leather strap as a Confirmation gift. It resembles the one she wears. It is shaped like two wooden nails intersecting.

My parents gave me money for my trip to New York with Grandma Iris.

My grandmothers were at my Confirmation. They were very competitive for attention, as usual. I think it is sweet.

Mo wanted to be at my Confirmation but his family had an anniversary celebration. I think it was better that way.

Mo would have enjoyed Bishop Wright slapping me. Well, it's not like a slap when someone is mad at you.

It is like sending a soldier off to battle and saying, "Peace be with you" with a smack to the face. Plus, the Confirmed are blessed with holy oils.

We all were wondering how hard Bishop Wright would slap. It wasn't real hard, but it still made me want to react.

I think Mo would have followed the bishop around afterward. The bishop wasn't there very long, so that would have disappointed Mo.

I really enjoyed the celebration afterward. These are the moments that make me happy, having my family together.

I wish Anny were alive to be there. She would have been so emotional, but happy.

April 18, 2007

I got a car today!! My parents surprised me for my birthday.

It is an old lady car. A used car my dad found in a classified ad.

It is super clean. A garage kept car.

I love it!

It is a 1999 silver Honda Civic with 40,000 miles.

We went over to the church and Father Murphy blessed the car inside and out. He has blessed all our cars.

I can't wait to show Mo!

I expect Michael will eventually ride in the backseat with my dad. Ha! Ha!

Michael is like ten feet tall and those wings are crazy huge, but he manages to fit into small cars.

I want to personalize my car, but I don't want bumper stickers. I <u>do</u> want a custom license plate.

I wish I could reupholster the interior in a rich red plaid.

I'd also put green felt in the back window with a white architectural drawing of New York. I don't know why that came to me, but I really like the idea.

I'd also try to figure out how to put some reading lights in the backseat for my passengers. Not that my friends like to read much. But I just love the idea.

The outside I'm less concerned about.

I just want the interior to be my world. A place that I enjoy.

My parents won't let me drive to Tampa yet. There is a drive-in movie theater there and I want to go so bad!

My parents told me I am restricted to only driving in our immediate Pinellas County area.

I am also not allowed to cross bridges to Hillsborough County or go over the Skyway Bridge!

That's okay.

There's plenty to do around here. Once I am more experienced, I will go greater distances.

I have to pay for my own gas and insurance, so I need to budget.

April 24, 2007

Grandma Iris bought our tickets to New York!! This was the best birthday ever. We leave on Friday and come back Sunday night. She bought tickets for two shows!

I can't wait to see Central Park and eat New York pizza and go to Times Square!

Mom said Grandma will also take me to St. Patrick's Cathedral for mass.

April 25, 2007

I went shopping for some clothes for the trip. I got some new jeans, running shoes, and a dress for one fancy dinner. Grandma Iris wants to take me to Sardi's after one of the shows. She said that actors sometimes go there after their shows.

I can't wait!

April 27, 2007

Grandma and I flew to New York this morning. We landed at LaGuardia and I was so amazed to see everything from so far up.

The city looked like game pieces all packed in together. It was so exciting.

We took a taxi to the Waldorf Astoria, which is near St. Patrick's Cathedral and walking distance to Times Square and the theater district.

Grandma said we would maybe go to Radio City Music Hall. I can't wait to go to the Empire State Building!

April 28, 2007

We are seeing Legally Blonde tomorrow and an Off-Broadway matinee today called Her Bicycle.

We also took a tour bus all over the city.

I'm fascinated by all the architecture, especially the Flat Iron Building. The fact that someone designed it and it got built amazes me!

I convinced Grandma to eat a slice of pizza while standing!

She thinks it is uncivilized to stand at a counter and eat like there is a fire, she said.

AND she liked the pizza.

Mission accomplished!

We also toured St. Patrick's Cathedral and went to one of the daily masses.

April 29, 2007

We called Mom and Dad from our room phone at the Waldorf and I got to tell them all the things we were seeing. I didn't talk much because it is expensive and Grandma wanted to have a cocktail downstairs before the theater.

I never want to leave New York.

More later.

Continued

We went to Ground Zero and saw the World Trade Center cross.

That was a wake-up call, as Anny would say.

The cross was found after the 9/11 attack. It is actually a few beams from the World Trade Center towers that form a cross.

There was an aura around the cross. Unlike anything I've experienced before.

I then realized why God brought me to New York.

Sure, it's a chance to spend time with Grandma Iris, but it's a reminder to write the vision.

I asked Grandma if we could go back to St. Patrick's and she totally understood.

We stayed at the cathedral for hours. Grandma sat by me the whole time in prayer. She didn't question.

We went to dinner later and skipped the show.

I asked my Grandma why I have these feelings of the future as I do?

She said she didn't know, but if I am called by God (and she knows that I am) then we are just to trust.

I didn't tell her about Michael or the actual vision.

Grandma knows Sister Jo, and she knows that most teenagers don't hang out in cathedrals when they could be doing other things. She told me not to doubt, doubt is the devil's work.

Grandma also said that my guardedness is a sign that I am following God's will.

She said a prideful and boastful person would go around telling people what they know—to seek attention and acceptance from others.

That is not how she sees me.

She said she is delighted by me and will always be there for me.

I told her I think I'm supposed to live in New York, because I can't fulfill the mission anywhere else.

She said she'd pray for that.

May 1, 2007

I decided to just reflect and not write any more during my time in New York.

The trip home to Florida was quiet.

I watched the city from the plane and wondered how those poor people on 9/11 spent their final moments.

I felt like I was in a flying coffin.

I can't help but feel immense sadness, knowing that others have flown captive. But I believe they were in the company of angels.

May 11, 2007

I accidentally broke Dr. Bartlett's animal mold.

I didn't do it on purpose. I was filing and tripped. My sneaker stuck to the newly waxed floors.

Everything was tossed!

I knocked over the box containing the mold, a stack of files and a five-gallon jug of water that thankfully didn't burst.

The file contents spread out like dominoes in a long trail across the floor.

I couldn't grab them in time.

Anyway, the mold shattered to a green paste on the floor.

I inhaled a little of the green dust and coughed up a storm. I then drank two huge glasses of water to clear my throat.

Dr. Bartlett yelled out, "You didn't."

He had a patient in the chair and was going over their x-rays.

With a scratchy voice, I yelled, "Sorry."

Dr. Bartlett continued with his patient and when they were done he found me in the records room sweeping.

"Was that?" He said.

"The demon mold," I said, still a little hoarse.

I suddenly realized what I said.

He then started to laugh slowly. Then he kept laughing harder and harder.

I was a little worried for him. I thought he was going to choke at one point.

When he settled down he said, "Blair, you have an amazing sense of humor."

I said, "No really. I think it was a demon."

"You're serious?" He said.

I nodded, yes.

Then he started laughing even harder.

I reminded him that the doctor before him died of a heart attack before he finished the case.

He told me to stop, because he might die laughing.

He got on the phone with the lawyer who sent him the case and told him what I said. They both laughed for way too long!

I don't care. I am just glad the thing is gone.

May 12, 2007

Today I have a headache and my throat is still scratchy. I guess I'm getting a cold.

I sure hope it doesn't have anything to do with the green dust I inhaled.

Just writing this down to remind myself, in case I get to feeling worse.

Dr. Bartlett would crack up if he read this.

May 13, 2007

I had another God-flash.

I was in a tunnel and it was super dark. I felt a presence—like when I was in the antique shop. But it was more than one ghost. They were not making sense and I couldn't do anything to help them.

But the ghosts were somehow insisting that I do something. I don't know how I understood them, but that was the message.

I couldn't see them either. It was the worst feeling ever.

Being blind.

I wondered if it was hell.

I wondered if I was blind?

That's when I returned from the God-flash. All I could think was: I should tell Jo about the demon.

May 15, 2007

Mo has a girlfriend!

His family loves her because their families are culturally from the same region.

Farah is so beautiful. Her skin is lighter than Mo's. Her hair is the silkiest blackish brown I've ever seen. I can't describe it. It is hard to look away from her. You just want to stare.

Mo said they met at a friend's wedding.

I am so happy for them.

Farah seems to be a bit of a beautiful geek, so they are perfect for each other.

We all tried to hang out and have pizza, but I got uncomfortable with all their playful touching.

I wanted to hit Mo.

Like, don't gross me out!

I'm super happy for them, but I can't be around them.

I excused myself and went to the restroom.

I walked halfway home after.

They never noticed my leaving the restaurant.

Mo eventually called me and asked where I went. I told him I walked home. He was disappointed.

I felt bad, because I didn't say goodbye to Farah.

I guess I was rude.

May 17, 2007

I told Jo about the demon that Michael pulled out of her.

She didn't doubt me. I thought she was going to.

I even thought she'd suggest a psychiatric evaluation or something like that, but she didn't.

I told her I was afraid to tell her about the demon, but she explained that if Michael honored her by his protection and I witnessed it—why would she disbelieve?

I cried like a baby.

She also told me she has stage-four breast cancer.

I didn't know what to say.

Here I was worried about telling her *how Michael saved her* and she tells me she has stage-four cancer.

She also told me to get serious and discern what God wants me to do about the vision.

I said I didn't know what I would do without her. She is literally the only person who understands me.

She said that my parents understand me, that my grandmothers understand and even Father Murphy now understands me.

I felt like she was saying goodbye.

She had tears in her eyes, but she didn't cry or get upset.

She said our calling is to accept what God brings into our life.

When I left, I promised I'd work on the discernment.

In a way, I wish I hadn't gone. I don't want to think about any of this. I love her and want her to be well.

May 18, 2007

When I told my parents about Sister Jo's cancer, we all cried. We also agreed to start a novena for her and dad said he'd participate, too.

I also told them about the discernment and how she wants me to decide what God is calling me to do.

They trust Sister Jo.

They said for me to let them know.

That I can tell them anything.

May 19, 2007

The 22nd is the last day of school. It is such a relief the school year is ending.

I don't know how to feel about anything.

I feel like all my friends are leaving me, which means I guess I should find new friends and relationships and start thinking about college.

I don't know what I want to do?

I am going to drive to the beach to spend time in prayer.

May 20, 2007

I went to a prayer service just before the beach last night. I wrote down the readings and they align with my discernment.

It was so overwhelmingly obvious! Not code or anything.

Job 1:6–8

One day the heavenly beings came to present themselves before the Lord, and Satan also came among them. The Lord said to Satan, "Where have you come from?" Satan answered the Lord, "From going to and fro on the earth, and from walking up and down on it."

Ephesians 5:15–20

Be careful then how you live, not as unwise people but as wise, making the most of the time, because the days are evil.

Matthew 24:42–47

Jesus said, "Keep awake therefore, for you do not know on what day your Lord is coming. But understand this: if the owner of the house had known in what part of the night the thief was coming, he would have stayed awake and would not have let his house be broken into. Therefore you also must be ready, for the Son of Man is coming at an unexpected hour.

I fell asleep at the beach and the water rushed up to grab me. I was lying on the sand looking up at the stars when I began my evening.

I felt like a zombie.

I remember counting in my head. I count when I can't think.

The noise of the waves gave me peace.

I wondered (looking up at the stars) how I could be in possession of a message for a girl in the future?

At what point, will she look for an answer and find what I provide?

Where am I to put the vision?

On what do I put the vision? A letter, a Word document, a pdf, a blog post or video?

Michael is a messenger; Gabriel is a messenger and I am not a heavenly being!

Then John the Baptist came to mind and I realized that he, too, was a human messenger and not angelic.

But I can't compare myself.

Then I thought of the Ephesians reading and realized that Paul, too was called, though an enemy.

Also, none of these guys are female.

Mary the mother of Jesus was the first disciple of Christ. She gave birth to him! Though this is my interpretation.

They say Jesus was the new Adam and Mary the new Eve, so is Sybille the new Paul? But she isn't an enemy I don't think?

So where do I fit in?

Would that make me the new Ananias?

I looked up Paul's conversion from Saul to Paul.

Acts 9:10-12

Now there was a disciple in Damascus named Ananias. The Lord said to him in a vision, "Ananias." He answered, "Here I am, Lord." The Lord said to him, "Get up and go to the street called Straight, and at the house of Judas look for a man of Tarsus named Saul. At this moment he is praying, and he has seen in a vision a man named Ananias come in and lay his hands on him so that he might regain his sight."

Sight seems to be a key sense in God's messaging. Seeing is believing?

Thomas was unable to believe until he saw Jesus' wounds...

Are we blind to the truth? Until something gives us clarity?

I'm doubting again.

Or am I just trying to draw comparisons to my visions?

But I know Paul!

Does everything have to be justified with the past?

I will be the past in Sybille's future.

Then the waves rushed up and woke me.

I thought at first that I was at the park and a gator creeped up from the lake to pull me in.

Then sand washed away under me and I thought perhaps I was sinking into the lake's muck and I jumped.

I opened my eyes and saw the moon and desperately crab crawled backward.

My mind didn't connect where I was.

Once I realized it was the beach, I settled down.

I looked behind me and saw lights on in a beach cottage. Did anyone see me?

I figured if someone was watching, they were likely having a good laugh, since they could see the advancing waves.

Nothing made sense until I got home and started writing this down.

I then realized...

I've been writing to Sybille all along in this diary!

The diary is the mode of my message!

The vision belongs here, in this diary, or perhaps a new diary to Sybille?

But where will she find it?

Where will I place it?

Dear Lord, provide me a clue.

May 22, 2007

Today was the last day of school. We signed each other's yearbooks and talked about our summer plans. It seemed like we'd never see each other again. Weird.

Sister Jo came to our house for dinner tonight.

She was very happy and animated. Very different.

We were so excited for her! She seemed to be healing and looked good!

My parents commented that her happiness displayed improved health.

Then she gave us the news.

We couldn't believe it!

She said that she was leaving the church and her order to join a secular organization that has roots in our city.

The Apostasy.

My parents were super wigged out. I didn't know much about The Apostasy until Mom went crazy on Sister Jo.

I learned that it has been around for years, and has begun to grow faster since young celebrities have joined.

The Apostasy also offers motivation seminars for corporate clients. Mom said the seminars are mostly an attempt to draw faith believers away from their religion to one of self-reliance.

They market self-help and self-love. To pledge membership, one must give up material possessions to the organization.

Members are then moved into The Apostasy communal housing to work and their children are educated at the organization's schools.

The rich who join The Apostasy pledge their holdings in exchange for hotel-style living at the organization's more lavish properties.

The elite then live with other like-minds and grow The Apostasy as part of the agreement.

Sister Jo used to be an executive.

I asked how she could change her beliefs?

She said it was a perfect fit for her. She had already taken a vow of poverty with the church, and this was no different.

She said she would rather live in a community than in her apartment. Her faith served her well, but now she was physically dying, her vision diminishing and she wanted to offer The Apostasy her corporate and Catholic experience.

As a workaholic who had lived in isolation before she became a nun, Jo said she understood how to teach non-believers to be self-sufficient.

She felt honored that The Apostasy wanted her. "To bring the religious in."

My mother got super angry!

"Why on earth would you betray God in this way?!" she asked.

Jo calmly replied, "Have you clothed the naked? Fed the hungry? Visited the imprisoned? Sheltered the homeless?"

My mother knew Jo had her.

Jo went on.

The Apostasy does this for society's cast-offs: the poor, the homeless, the addicted, the lonely and the lost. They bring them into the fold.

My mother's eyes got big, "They take in the homeless and train them to take care of the rich! The Apostasy is a labor camp!"

Jo didn't deny it. "Would you rather the poor starve in the streets? Even our church has failed them at times."

Mom got indignant, "Our charities help more people worldwide than any other church. Yes, maybe I have failed the homeless, but it doesn't give an organization the right to enslave them for free labor!"

Jo was so calm that you could feel a chill settle over the room.

"They come of their own free will. Let's face it, there is a fight for souls. Whose soul are you saving?" Jo asked mom.

Dad kept quiet. He was clearly not sure what to say.

He muttered, "Souls..."

And then I snapped at Jo and words flew out before I could think them, "Yes, we **are** in a fight for souls and <u>**yours**</u> is one!"

Mom looked to dad. They were troubled.

Jo said to me, "Let's enjoy this meal together."

Mom then settled down and asked Jo to say a blessing over the meal.

Jo instead excused herself to go to the restroom and we prayed without her and for her.

I believe Jo has a serious battle within.

There must be a remnant of the demon in her. None of this made any sense?!

After dinner, I sprinkled some holy water on my hands when no one was looking. I went to hug Jo, but she rejected me.

She said it was time to be self-reliant and she no longer wanted affection.

However, she said I could visit her at The Apostasy.

I touched her anyway.

She stared at me in the most frightening way.

I can't describe it.

If my parents hadn't been there; I think she would have strangled me.

My parents couldn't see what I saw.

I told Jo that I would continue to pray for her and she turned quickly and thanked my parents for the meal and left.

May 23, 2007

I couldn't sleep last night.

I'm a teenager, going into the summer of my 16th year. I have a car, but I don't know where to go or what to do.

I had a dream about New York. I thought about my trip with Grandma Iris and then I started thinking about Jo and my vision.

The Apostasy is weighing on me and I just don't know how this fits into my mission?

I'm going to drive by The Apostasy headquarters and pray for the people inside and those walking around the city.

I think I'm going to ask Mo to join me.

If he still wants to transition to the faith, this is the time.

May 25, 2007

Yesterday was a great day.

It was so much fun to hang with Mo and joke like we used to.

We drove by The Apostasy and shouted at the security guards to let the people go. They ignored us.

I almost had an accident. Mo jumped into the backseat and held up a handmade sign in the back window that read: The Apostasy is EVIL.

I almost hit one of their members looking at Mo in the rearview mirror.

When I hit the brakes, Mo fell backwards and landed on the floor. He cracked up laughing.

All I could think of was Michael and my Driver's Ed class. Maybe my guardian angel was in the front seat with me?

I wonder who was protecting the person I almost hit.

The Apostasy member and the guards outside didn't seem to think much of our commotion.

I guess it isn't unusual for protesters to shout at them or hold up signs.

Mo and I then went to Sand Key Beach and joked about our teachers and what they will be doing this summer. We wanted to make sand angels, but decided it would be too itchy.

Mo said he loves Farah and his parents think she is perfect. He didn't dwell on it.

I am happy for him.

He asked my advice on things he could do for Farah's birthday.

We've grown up.

Mo has more facial hair. Gained more confidence. And is ready to drive.

I think we'll always be friends. Maybe I'll be a godmother to one of his kids. I know I want kids, but I wonder if I'll ever have any?

I certainly wouldn't want to have a kid like me… that has visions and doesn't know how to be a kid.

Don't get me wrong. I would not reject a kid who had these gifts. I'd be the right mother for a kid who did. But it isn't a kid's life.

May 26, 2007

I told my parents I need to live in New York. I just can't do this anymore.

My parents listened and agreed. They said the whole thing with Sister Jo and my visions convinced them their calling is to support me and even if we must scrap all we own, if we are together, it will be okay.

Mom is afraid of snow, though. She at first said we should think about whether we should uproot ourselves.

She hasn't lived in the cold and worries how we'll manage. Dad told her to 'surrender, for God's sake' and we all laughed.

It seems we all have doubts about our strengths and weaknesses.

We went to the office supply store and got a For Sale By Owner sign and put it in the yard.

Neighbors we've never met came to inquire.

Mom was sad that we had not been as neighborly as we could have been. She regretted that it took a sign to get us all out of our houses and talk.

Then dad said, you are always saying you want a sign from God, well, you got it!

We can be neighborly in New York.

June 1, 2007

I gave my notice to Dr. Bartlett today.

Grandma Iris said she would help us.

I also told Mo. He wants to go with us, but his parents won't let him.

Also, he has Farah! I reminded him of that.

Mo likes adventure, so I almost think he would give up Farah just to travel. Crazy.

Also, he can't join us, he would distract me.

Grandma Iris said she would come up occasionally to go to shows with me.

I am so amazed my family is this supportive and willing to make a change for the sake of my calling.

Everyone thinks I'll become a nun at some point, but I don't have that kind of calling.

Bishop Wright contacted St. Patrick's Cathedral on our behalf to let them know we are moving up.

Father Murphy wants me to have another spiritual director in New York.

I'm kinda scared.

Scared that my family will go broke moving and scared that I'm not going to get this right.

I must keep praying.

June 11, 2007

We got our first offer on the house and my parents were surprised.

We have been cleaning, packing, painting and the bid was under our asking price.

Mom said if it had been our asking price we'd have to move immediately.

Grandma Iris said we could live at her house if we needed for a month or so if the house goes quickly.

I'm okay sleeping on a couch or even in a sleeping bag in the car if necessary. I just want this to be over.

I'm wondering where the heck Michael is?

Here I am following his direction and he isn't even guiding me.

We're going to sell my car, next.

I am seriously bummed about it. It is such a sweet car, but we won't need it in the city.

Whoever buys it gets a blessed car.

We now have a sign on my car and a sign in the yard.

My dad is going to leave our family car at Grandma Iris' so we have a car to use when we visit. He said he may sell it, too. But for the time being, it may be helpful to have a vehicle here.

June 15, 2007

I took a bag of clothing to the church as a donation for the migrant ministry.

Father Murphy was there and asked me to come into his office and chat.

He said he wanted me to know that the 'storm day' mass was a test for both of us.

He said that God speaks to all of us in his own way if we are listening.

I wanted to tell him about the day Michael blocked him from leaving. The day Sister Jo was possessed, but I knew in my heart these were not words to be spoken.

Whatever Father Murphy was acknowledging, was the extent of what he felt was his duty as a pastor and priest.

He asked me to pray for Sister Jo and I told him I was.

I asked him how we as a church could stand up to The Apostasy.

He said we must pray for those who don't know Christ, those who harm the faithful, those who want to separate us from our faith and those who have left the church.

It was the first time I felt we connected. That he understood me and didn't think of me as a little kid or dumb teenager.

I don't think adults realize how they make kids feel sometimes. But I was happy we did have time to talk and he said a blessing over me before I left.

I think he understood that I miss Sister Jo.

I don't understand how she could turn on the church.

Could I have done something?

Did she need an exorcist?

Should I go back and ask Father Murphy?

Should I tell him everything?

I know the bishop helped Sister Jo come off the streets...

Something is not making sense, or is it?

Devil get behind me!

I've got to pray.

June 29, 2007

We sold the house.

We've been so busy packing and cleaning that I've not had a chance to write.

I am excited to be moving.

Mo and Farah came over and we had a pizza party on the living room floor. It was funny. My parents joined us and afterward we took some pictures, so that we would have these memories.

I don't know why we haven't done this more often.

I wish there were more pictures. We have mostly birthday party photos and Christmas gift-opening photos. But it isn't like when my parents were growing up.

We have albums of photos of my parents and grandparents doing all kinds of things. Like barn raising, milking cows, walking down the city streets, playing baseball and vacationing.

Why don't we take these types of photos now? Everything is posed.

All the ancient old-time photos are of people in a photo studio as an individual or group. When cameras weren't portable.

Why do we pose now, when we could take photos of people doing things?

As we evolve, we also come full circle as Granny says.

July 4th, 2007

We are living with Grandma Iris until we have our place in New York.

We all went to Granny's, including Grandma Iris to see the fireworks.

Granny's condo has a great view of the Gulf of Mexico and it was enchanting to watch the lights reflect off the water.

I stayed in Granny's guest room tonight.

At Grandma Iris's I sleep on the sofa bed, so a real bed feels good.

I was thinking about Christmas in July!

I always do this. Think of other holidays instead of the holiday we are celebrating.

Well, I saw 'Christmas in July' ads on TV tonight and it got me thinking.

Our religion teaches that Mary was the Immaculate Conception, meaning that her mother St. Anne conceived Mary without the stain of original sin.

Original sin is the sin of Eve tempting Adam and their both eating the fruit from the tree of knowledge in the Garden of Eden (as tempted by the serpent). A lot of tempting...

So, if Mary was conceived without sin, that means God had to prepare her mother Anne's womb for Mary. Then God would also prepare Mary's womb for Jesus?

That is a lot of planning for God and giving Anne and Mary free will was a total act of trust. Right?

Seems like a stretch.

Why would you need Jesus if these two women are perfect?

Most people think the Immaculate Conception is Mary conceiving Jesus without knowing a man. Yet it is the Incarnation that refers to God becoming a human in the womb of Mary as the Angel Gabriel foretold.

I think Mary's yes to conceiving Jesus through the Holy Spirit would have purified her womb and St. Anne wouldn't have had to conceive Mary without sin.

I think our humanity desires that Mary be as we are, imperfect and stained with Original sin.

To think that any woman could be the mother of Jesus by her willingness to receive the gift of the Holy Spirit and be an instrument in salvation history is the epitome of sacrifice, awe and reverence.

I would like to think that St. Anne was a good mother, but it is hard to accept that God would prepare her womb for Mary, when he only needed to prepare Mary's at the moment of conception, for Jesus.

Mary said yes.

Could another woman say yes and erase the wrong of Eve and give birth to the savior?

Eve was perfect. Until her fall from grace.

Mary technically should not be perfect, because she is as much Eve's daughter as her mother Anne.

If Jesus can be in the line of David, of which there is no direct bloodline, because his foster father Joseph is in the line of David, then Mary could be a sweet virgin from a good family and be deemed full of grace at the moment she says, "let it be done to me according to your word."

Then the word became flesh in the conception of Jesus and, Mary's womb purified at that moment.

I looked up some references and it seems there are historical differences on Mary's being sinless at her birth.

I think God wants that to be a mystery.

Why else would he have forbidden Adam and Eve from eating the fruit from the tree of knowledge?

Maybe there was another tree he wanted to nourish them? Maybe the tree of wisdom?

Wow!

I think I discovered the first junk food, the fruit of the tree of knowledge!

July 12, 2007

The New York realtor called. She is having trouble finding us something in our price range and it is hard to tell what the neighborhoods look like from the photos she is sending us. None of us know the city well enough to understand. Dad has a job interview with a janitorial company and we're thinking that one of us should go with him.

Instead, mom and I came up with an idea. We could drive up to New Jersey and stay some place cheap and take a bus or train into the city when the realtor has something for us to see.

Dad doesn't like the idea. He said we should just move into a hotel room in New York and start working with the realtor until we find our place.

Dad's worried we'll spend too much time traveling from New Jersey to get to the realtor appointments.

He's probably right.

August 20, 2007

I saw an Apostasy ad on TV today and it made me furious. They were trying to appeal to young people who have insecurities.

I am not sure how to deal with this. I will pray about it, but I feel an urging to do something, but I don't know what?

August 30, 2007

Dad got the janitor job and moved up to New York this week. It is so lonely living like we are. I feel like maybe we made a mistake. Like I'm going to tear my family apart with the visions.

But I know we'll all be fine when we are living together. I really hope that once I get the diary in place, I will be able to go to college and start over.

Hit a reset button.

September 14, 2007

Mom and I moved from Tampa, Florida to Manhattan.

Dad found an affordable hotel.

I am exploring the city to find where Sybille would live.

It is a very distracting task.

My instincts guide me in these situations.

I don't know how it works, but I get a feeling that envelopes me and my brain feels tight the closer I get to where I am supposed to be.

I have no illness.

It is a sensation.

Michael believes my gifts may weaken once I have fulfilled the mission.

I really want to be done with this chapter of my life.

More tomorrow.

Sept 15, 2007

St. Patrick's Cathedral feels like a hotbed of activity.

Not from the people who are coming and going to the daily masses and the tourists, but there is a field of negative energy outside.

I sat on the steps for hours.

I'm praying whatever it is will go away. I'm not sure where it is, what it is or if it is happening now or is part of the vision. I know something is going to happen there.

I hoped Michael would appear at some point. He seems to leave me alone more. I guess this is part of the process.

I don't like it.

It is an awful feeling.

Oct 10, 2007

Today was better.

I grabbed a slice of pizza at the same place where Grandma and I ate on our visit.

I feel comfortable there.

It is hard to feel alone with so many people around.

I listen to what people are talking about and it is fascinating.

Plus, the pizza's sooo good. One giant slice with loads of gooey cheese. Heaven.

I think I could eat this every day.

The shop owner smiled at me when he saw how much I enjoyed it.

I said to him, "The best!"

He nodded as he flipped a circle of dough above his head.

It made me realize how much we need those little moments of appreciation and recognition.

His smile gave me a feeling of connection.

Could we end wars and stop hate with simple gratitude?

Oct 13, 2007

The vibe at the Empire State Building is almost electric. When I'm inside, I'm nauseous.

I know this is a place of importance.

The nausea is warning sign.

Sister Jo helped me identify this a while back.

This feels very different.

I'm just not sure why?

I'm so overwhelmed that this is as much as I can write.

Oct 21, 2007

My new spiritual director got sick. I'm glad. I don't want a man as a spiritual director. I am going to go without.

I think I'm in the right place and I understand what I need to do.

Nov 10, 2007

I'm attending Basilica Catholic High School which is far away from the hotel where we live. It isn't next to St. Patrick's.

You'd think it would be.

They take all nationalities and faiths.

I didn't want to go to Catholic school, but Father Murphy back home said a church member made a gift in their will for me to attend a Catholic school. Father Murphy told my parents after we got here.

Strange how things happen.

We aren't allowed to know who.

Anyway, I take the subway to school. I am glad I wear a uniform.

It makes me invisible.

No one pays attention to anyone on the subway, but it seems that a uniform just adds a layer of sameness.

At school, we keep talking about a free day, when we get to wear our regular clothes. It is a part of a fundraiser.

Weird that the students want to wear their regular clothes to school.

We all are required to participate in the school fundraiser.

We have to sell chocolate bars and if we reach our goal, we get a free day to wear our own clothes.

Right now, I'm painting bright colors on my sneakers and jeans for art class so maybe I'll wear that on free day.

My new friend Athena is Greek Orthodox. She wants our uniforms redesigned. Her mother works in the garment district and

Athena wants to be a designer. Her father owns a small restaurant in Queens.

I asked Athena if she believed in the church and God.

It seems a lot of kids don't.

She said that she loves the Orthodox church and traditions, but thinks everyone has missed the hidden messages in the bible.

Athena thinks Mary was the Messiah.

Athena said since men were in power during the Old and New Testament, of course they wouldn't let a woman be recorded as a Messiah.

Athena said Mary was the real Messiah, because God impregnated her.

That blew my mind.

We talked about it for a long time.

Athena thinks that Jesus' sacrifice was like completing Abraham's mission to sacrifice Isaac, but more to test Mary, too.

Mary let Jesus die.

She knew things.

She knew Jesus could turn water into wine before he did.

That is why you barely find anything about her in the bible, Athena thinks.

Abraham was tested, too.

Athena said that Isaac being strapped to wood is the symbol.

Like Jesus, Issac was to be sacrificed on wood.

But since God had destined Abraham's descendants to be as vast as the stars, Isaac had to live.

God knew Jesus would be his backup Isaac.

Athena said that Mary, unlike Abraham and Sarah who were his instruments, was the Messiah.

Isaac, too is a son of God in Athena's thinking. Because God fathered Isaac. Too much to explain here.

I must say, she is very convincing in her arguments. She should become a politician.

I enjoyed the discussion.

I also wonder if she has experienced anything supernatural, or is just into conspiracies?

We'll see.

Nov 15, 2007

We're still selling chocolates and I've eaten more than I have sold. I am beginning to hate chocolate.

My Dad took some to work with him, but they never made it. He left them on the subway.

We're paying for that box and the ones I've eaten. It seems irresponsible for the school to give us so much freedom with a temptation.

I guess everyone isn't tempted. But then again, kids love candy. This isn't right!

Nov 16, 2007

The archbishop was in today, this is our last school day before Thanksgiving break.

Athena and I got into trouble.

Athena wanted to challenge the archbishop on her theory that God impregnated Sarah, Abraham's wife.

She shouted out, "Blair wants to ask bishop a question" when we were in assembly.

Everyone got quiet and stared in our direction. I was totally weirded out with all these eyes staring at us.

Athena was in her glory.

Our principal gave us **the look!**

Then our teacher removed us from the assembly.

The archbishop paused at first like he wanted to hear us out, but noticed the way Athena was snickering.

I deeply regret my association with her.

We both were kept after school to clean chalkboards, erasers and desk tops. I didn't mind the cleaning, but Athena wouldn't shut up or work!

While I cleaned, she took out her bible and read:

Genesis 21:1-2

The Lord visited Sarah as he had said, and the Lord did to Sarah as he promised. And Sarah conceived, and bore Abraham a son in his old age at the time of which God had spoken to him.

Athena said that Sarah and Mary had moments where they technically weren't supposed to have a baby and they were in opposite situations and God impregnated them.

Sarah was old and barren and Mary a virgin who had not known a man sexually.

Athena thinks that God stopped Abraham from burning Isaac because it was really His kid, not Abraham's, but Mary had to finish what Abraham didn't. Because God knew He disrupted his own universe.

That really had me thinking.

Because Athena said Mary had to let her son die.

Athena also said that if Abraham is the father of multitudes as written in Genesis 17:5 then Mary is in line with Sarah.

Which didn't make sense somehow.

I challenged Athena. I asked how Mary is a Messiah and in the line of Sarah?

Athena drew out a scene on my newly cleaned chalk board.

Then she read aloud:

Genesis 17:15-16

And God said to Abraham, "As for Sar'ai your wife, you shall not call her name Sar'ai, but Sarah shall be her name.

I will bless her, and moreover and I will give you a son by her; I will bless her, and she shall be a mother of nations; kings of peoples shall come from her."

I asked Athena, why doesn't the bible give Mary's lineage?

Because Jesus is in the line of King David and Joseph, who isn't his father.

Athena got frustrated with me.

She said that men weren't going to give Mary a past or future, beyond being the mother of Jesus.

She called me stupid.

But she still didn't answer the question either.

I wanted to cover her in chalk dust, but I don't want to have to spend more time with her...

Nov 19, 2007

Don't ask me why, but I agreed to hang out with Athena today. I may be as stupid as she says I am.

We met at her family's diner and they fed us.

That was worth it!

We ate at the counter.

I tried spinach pie and stuffed grape leaves. I liked the spinach pie the best.

Athena's family is super nice. I really like their diner. It is long and narrow.

There is a row of booths by the window and a long counter opposite the booths.

All the customers seem to be regulars.

I like the Italians and Greeks. They rag on each other a lot!

I offered to help wash dishes and Athena kicked me.

She is such a spoiled brat.

Her father asked if I was coming to Athena's sleepover.

Athena rolled her eyes.

I caught her reflection off the mirror behind the counter.

Athena then changed the subject. Out of the blue she said to me, "Wait a minute, you're a medium!"

I don't see myself like that. I've always thought of mediums as people who aren't Godly. If I am, Athena will exploit me.

Athena really loves intrigue and drama! If she expanded her thinking, she'd see there is plenty of supernatural mystery in the world.

I didn't acknowledge or discourage Athena, I just let her go on about this medium thing.

Was that wrong?

Should I have said that I'm not a medium?

I'm not sure what I am.

Nov 20, 2007

Athena's mom had to work today. She is finishing something for a client, so Athena and I went with to her job.

The garment manufacturing plant is so cool. I love the messy scraps of fabric and thread littering the floor.

The building where Athena's mom works has been around for more than 100 years.

There were a few other people working. Athena also sat down to sew and no one cared. I just sat next to her and watched.

I wish my mom had a cool job. She does data entry at a bank. Boring!

Athena made us both a gray knit tank top and matching fingerless gloves in a few minutes. I was so impressed!

Afterward, we modeled them and wore them to grab an ice cream on our way home.

As we were walking to the subway, I asked Athena if she ever experienced visions or the presence of the angels or saints.

Athena stopped and looked at me like I was crazy!

Seriously!

She said, "Don't let the medium thing go to your head, I just wanted to see if you were game to having a séance."

She then laughed and said I'm super creepy.

I was so hurt. Stunned.

I wanted to run off.

Then she told me her family is moving to Tarpon Springs, Florida to take over her grandparents' restaurant once their Queens diner is sold.

I made an excuse and left quickly. I walked around the city for hours. When I got to the Hell's Kitchen district, I thought Athena should live there. I don't know the history of Hell's Kitchen, just that it must have been a bad place a long time ago.

I think Athena is a jerk.

I'm more determined than ever to write the vision.

Maybe that is why this happened. To get me back on track.

Nov 21, 2007

Tomorrow is Thanksgiving and me, mom and dad are going to the Macy's parade!

I'm helping my mom prepare some pies and casseroles today.

After we finish we're going to take a nap, then get up and go help Dad clean one of the office buildings along the parade route.

He works third shift and sleeps while I'm at school and mom is working.

We won't get any real rest, but we'll watch the Thanksgiving parade while our turkey breast cooks in the crock-pot.

I wish Granny and Grandma Iris would be able to join us.

I can't wait to see the parade live!

November 22, 2007 Thanksgiving

I am too tired to write. I'm sooo hungry!

Our turkey smells good, but we are so sleepy that we are not going to eat much. More tomorrow!

Nov 23, 2007

OK, about the parade...

After we helped Dad, we had a little extra time.

We had hot chocolate and bagels at a cart not far from Dad's job on Central Park West.

Then we walked to where the balloons are inflated.

It was magical.

I only wish I could have been one of the people to hold the strings and walk in the parade.

Everyone was so happy and friendly. I wish that moment could last forever.

Mom brought old blankets and comforters.

She ditched them after the parade, giving them to the homeless. These were extra layers we needed. We couldn't bring chairs, but took turns curling up, until more people showed up and there was no room along the sidewalks.

In the beginning, we sat back-to-back and stretched. We stood and took turns sitting and massaging each other's shoulders.

When the parade started, everyone had to lock into their position, because it was too crowded.

On one of the parade floats a singing group, Up With People, passed by.

Mom said she belonged to this organization when she was in college. She said their mission is to inspire young people to make a difference.

I really didn't understand how performing can help young people make a difference?

Dad and I cracked up. Mom didn't appreciate our imitations of her singing.

We wanted mom to sing for us and she said we weren't taking her seriously.

It was the best laugh I've had in forever.

Poor mom.

Dec 4th, 2007

Grandma Iris called and she will be coming up for Christmas!! She wants to go to Radio City Music Hall and maybe go ice skating with me.

Dad said his mother was a good ice skater. That she always wanted to be an Olympic figure skater. I am so happy she is coming up!

Dec 24th, 2007

Merry Christmas New York!

We went skating at Rockefeller Center today. I am not very graceful. I'm still learning how to ice skate. I pulled some little kids down when I was trying to grab for something to hold on to. I felt so bad. They told me to pick on someone my own size.

The Christmas decorations and holiday window displays in the city are amazing.

I haven't written for almost a month.

I decided to take time to meditate and pray.

I've been meditating on St. Paul's instruction to the Thessalonians.

1 Thessalonians 5:21

Do not treat prophecies with contempt, but test them all;
hold on to what is good, reject every kind of evil.

The vision is speaking to me and while I reject evil, as it relates, I know that without the vision, there will be no good.

BLAIR AT AGE 17

January 5, 2008

I found a building being renovated and I'm sure it is where Sybille will live.

There was an aura on the tenth floor and there I met a beautiful grandmother, Jewel Tallon, frantic to sublease her daughter-in-law's apartment.

Mrs. Tallon isn't yet a grandmother, but explained that her son Porter Tallon and his new wife Quinn are expecting a baby soon and they want her in Belfast for the delivery.

Mrs. Tallon asked if I was the individual who inquired about subleasing?

I laughed at her thinking a teenager could rent this place. A compliment to me, for sure.

Mrs. Tallon doesn't live in New York. She lives in... I'm not sure... I didn't ask. She said she took the train in.

Anyway, she is doing her son and his new bride a favor.

Mrs. Tallon's fair skin and brilliant red hair gave me an eerie feeling. I don't know what it is about her, or maybe it is something about the baby? I have a strange feeling.

I don't think the apartment is haunted, she did say that her son Porter had been extremely sick not long ago and that is how he met his wife Quinn. She was his aid at the hospital.

That's where they fell in love.

I'm not sure if she means Quinn is a nurse?

Anyway, Mrs. Tallon said that her son and daughter-in-law had eloped. That she wasn't going to miss the delivery of her only grandchild, given she wasn't there for their wedding.

Later I brought my parents to meet Mrs. Tallon. We'll be moving in next week.

The synchronicity of my finding the building, the gracious and strange Mrs. Tallon, and a fully furnished affordable rental is beyond belief.

We don't need to bring anything but our clothing and personal items when we move. How could it be this easy?

January 10, 2008

I feel so at peace in our new apartment.

I'm now able to focus.

We are in walking distance of St. Patrick's and Central Park with a beautiful view of the skyline. I can't stop looking out the window.

There is also a creaky old elevator in the building.

The old architecture is so enchanting.

I need to get to my homework.

February 3, 2008

Today my teacher said that the Book of Revelation was written in code by St. John for the people of his time.

However, if it is inspired, why would John write in code... and how is it still around for thousands of years (after the people of his time)?

I'm not one to believe that God would have us decode his word.

But I do know that scripture can only be understood when your mind is open to it.

I hope Sybille's mind is open to the vision when she reads it.

Not that I'm comparing myself to St. John or consider my writing to be sacred.

I do wonder sometimes about how things are taught and how they will be interpreted in the future.

Well, I guess that has been going on our whole human history.

February 6, 2008

It is Ash Wednesday and the city is full of smudged foreheads.

I think this is so cool!

Somehow, it is weird to think that Hitler had the Jewish people wear a Star of David to identify who was to be persecuted, instead of something disgraceful.

Not that I am giving the German any consideration at all.

But it does seem a symbol of God during a dark time was a way for our heavenly father to remind us that we belong to Him. That he is with us through it all.

Smudged crosses on the foreheads of Catholics on Ash Wednesday is the only day when you know who your real kin are.

That seems sad. Right?

For lent I'm not going to eat pizza for 40 days. That is going to be hard! I love grabbing a slice on my way home from school. The money I save, I'm going to put in the alms box at St. Patrick's.

Lent is about transformation, so I'm working on being a better me inside and out.

February 14, 2008

Weird that this year lent and Valentine's Day are so close.

Today is Valentine's Day and yes, I got sad watching all the couples looking content as they strolled to dinner or the theater.

Older men picking up flowers and candies for their wives make me happy. Their faces are so radiant and joyful.

Mom packed a card in with dad's lunch. I saw her sneak it in. Of course, Dad came home with roses for mom and a box of chocolates for me. My parents aren't fussy about big gifts.

They'll be cute old people.

I hope someday I'll be someone's someone.

March 8, 2008

I don't like Central Park after dark.

It just feels creepy in some sections, so with the clocks set forward an hour this weekend I'm going to take longer walks and I'm going to get mom to go with me. She always says she wants to exercise and now she won't have an excuse.

March 21, 2008 Good Friday

I'm not so sure why Good Friday is called Good Friday, since it was the day Jesus was crucified and died.

I mean, I looked up different meanings and I read that some thought good was a substitute word for holy.

So, if something is good, it is holy?

Do we strive to be good, or holy?

What if the whole world is good?

What does that imply?

Would the <u>whole</u> world be holy?

April 4, 2008

Granny got a cellphone and she called us. It is so funny. She kept hitting her speaker button and we could hear her bridge group asking her to turn her phone down.

We're not sure why she called when she was playing bridge, unless maybe someone was helping her?

She hung up on us a few times and we're not sure if she knows how to call back. But we all agree that if Grandma Iris finds out that Granny is more progressive than she is, she'll get a cellphone, too.

April 24, 2008

Finally, Michael shows up and of course it is Bring Your Daughter To Work Day!

I could only glare at him as he sat next to my mother and watched her type.

Seriously! I was furious.

So, I picked up my mother's stress ball and threw at him!

Of course, I missed.

Instead, I hit my mother in the back at the very moment her supervisor walked up to meet me.

Talk about awkward!

Michael quickly disappeared.

And to make matters worse, I rolled my eyes at Michael.

Then I turned and saw my mother's horrified expression.

From her point-of-view it looked like I was rolling my eyes at her boss.

Her supervisor smiled and muttered, "this is Blair?"

I just said, "Yo."

Then I heard myself say, "Yo."

I don't say yo!

Where did that come from?

Then Mom handed me a blank piece of paper and asked me to make her some copies. I looked at it and just walked to the restroom.

I hope my mother doesn't get fired.

She told me to go home before we could have lunch.

I felt bad. I know better.

May 5, 2008

I'll just call this Cinco de Michael-o day.

He showed up briefly. It has been a week or so since the last time I saw him.

He said he didn't have much time but wanted me to speed up my progress writing the vision.

I asked him about the demon he pulled from Sister Jo and told him how she joined The Apostasy. He just listened. He didn't offer up any clues.

I also wanted to know why he showed up at my mother's job.

He said, "Dependence on work has replaced faith."

He then asked me, "Why does your world want its daughters to be dependent on their employer?"

I thought that was odd. I don't think Michael understands women want to work.

After he left, I thought about Jo being a former workaholic and I guess that is what he is referring to?

You can't rely on your employer to be the answer to all your needs. Your purpose here is greater than the job you do, even if your job is your destiny.

What you do with your gifts is the purpose, not the wage earned. Right?

May 23, 2008

I got a job sweeping floors and cleaning restrooms at an off-Broadway theater. It doesn't have a name. It is a theater that is used by different groups and gets rented when a show producer has funds.

So far it is easy. I even get to watch some rehearsals when I'm done. Each cast and crew is different. Some are happy to have an audience member during the process and others don't want me there.

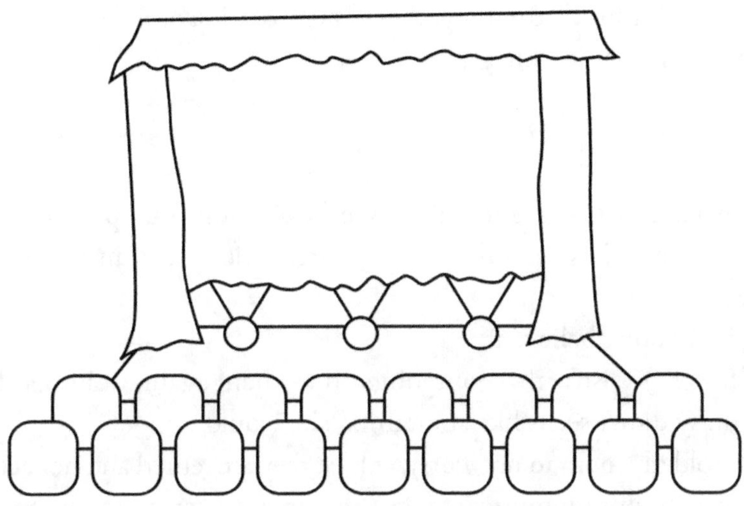

I'm not in their way, I just do my homework and watch when they are performing.

The Dominic, I call him, is the producer of a current show. He looks like Einstein and has a super loud voice when he talks to anyone.

Everything The Dominic says is of the utmost importance. His hands fly up, his eyes bulge and then his voice booms.

"Blair, we need more toilet paper in the restrooms!"

I nod and restock the bathrooms.

I feel like I should get applause whenever he asks me to do anything, because it feels like we are both performing.

Anyway, this job is like my old job working for Dr. Bartlett. Both jobs are about keeping things tidy and organized.

I need to start thinking about college. Though it seems to me the people who are clerks, waitresses, and laborers have way more interesting jobs than educated Wall Street bankers.

From my perspective, it seems like the higher the job title the phonier the life.

I watch people and listen.

The family-owned businesses seem to have more personality. The kids and the parents may fuss and argue, but they also laugh and spend a lot of time together. There is a lot of affection. They don't teach that in college.

June 1, 2008

Mom really wigged out today. She heard from our parish priest that Sister Jo has recruited some retired priests and nuns to join The Apostasy.

I just don't believe it.

Sister Jo isn't that outgoing, but then again, joining The Apostasy didn't seem like something she would do.

I told my mom to not worry, at least they are retired and not active in a parish. But mom is convinced that this is a covert operation.

She said, The Apostasy starts with the low hanging fruit, the retirees, homeless and work their way to the young people then the working class. It is all a matter of time.

I really don't know what they believe. It seems like a self-help group, but mom said there is more to it.

June 3, 2008

Today is the anniversary of my cousin Andi's death.

Up to about age seven, my life was fairly normal. Normal to me.

I was 8-years-old when I had a disturbing moment with my cousin.

I suddenly thought of her and got sick to my stomach.

My cousin Andi then appeared to me in a burst of sunshine that came through the curtains in my room while I was coloring.

Andi waved goodbye and at the same time my mother screamed like she was stabbed or something.

Mom got a call from my Aunt, Andi's mother.

That's how we got the news that Andi died.

Andi fell and hit her head playing at a friend's house. The concussion was thought to be minor.

They waited too long to take Andi to the hospital. Her brain swelled and she died.

That is my earliest memory of encountering the supernatural.

June 28, 2008

Mo called. He and Farah are touring colleges together and she is considering NYU.

Mo really doesn't know what he wants to do. He thinks that it is better to decide where you want to live and see what colleges in the area offer. Farah seems to be way more focused.

They are now in a serious relationship.

July 5, 2008

Athena is moving to Florida this week. I stayed at her house yesterday and we watched fireworks from the roof of the apartment building.

I really love her family!! Way more than Athena. They are so nice and tease Athena about being a brat. It cracks me up.

Anyway, we might visit their restaurant in Tarpon Springs next time we go home to visit Granny or Grandma Iris.

July 21, 2008

Mo and Farah stopped by before touring NYU. They didn't want to hang out. Farah looked like she had been crying. I'm not sure what happened. Mo was unsympathetic. I wanted to punch him for making her cry, but I realized that maybe he isn't to blame.

My parents were so happy Mo and Farah visited our apartment. Mom wanted to make dinner, but they left quickly.

August 7, 2008

We got a note from Mrs. Tallon, the lady who leased us her son's apartment. She said the baby was born, a boy named Clive.

I thought it was nice for her to let us know. It isn't like we know her.

Life is funny, you never really know why some people show up in your life.

She sent the letter with postage and no return address.

August 18, 2008

I went jogging in Central Park today and I saw the cutest little dog and his owner playing with a rubber ball. The dog was so happy and playful. I'm not sure I've ever seen a human or animal as happy and joyful as that little dog.

I wanted to scoop up that pup and take it home.

How can a little dog be that happy?

Why can't people be like that?

September 14, 2008

The news just announced that Wall Street collapsed!

At first I thought they were saying it was a terror attack and a building collapsed, but they were talking about our country's finances.

I'm not sure what it means.

My parents woke me and had me watch the news. They asked if this is part of the vision and I said, the vision is in the distant future.

They were frantic.

They wanted to know what they should do.

I felt bad.

I think they are uncertain what their roles are in bringing me into the world.

November 29, 2008

I stood at the apartment window today staring out at the city and a felt a nauseous wave of déjà vu.

I felt desperate.

I closed my eyes and audibly heard, "Need help."

I then leaned on the window sill and felt a tingling of electricity on my arm hairs.

I opened my eyes and looked out the window.

I'd seen this before!

In a God-flash!

Finally, I could match a place or moment with a God-flash!

But thankfully I wasn't on the outside ledge as I was in the flash.

I grabbed the window sill to steady myself and the board lifted slightly.

Now my heart was racing.

I gave the board a tug and looked inside the wall.

I saw a narrow gap in the insulation.

This is it!

My prayers have been answered.

This is where the diary belongs!

December 15, 2008

I am joining The Apostasy.

I now understand why Michael wanted me to write the vision while there was time.

I'm not sure if I will come out alive or if they will take control of my mind.

I must find Sister Jo if she is still alive.

If I accomplish nothing else, I will know that I did my best to help a friend break free from the demon who steered her away from God.

My mother begged me not to do this. She wants to go with me. She said she'd rather work with me than worry about me.

It took a lot of tears and discussion for her to accept that she has to let me go.

My parents understand the risk. I've asked them to trust that the angels and saints are with me through this. I am a soldier for Christ.

May God's will be done. I will return as is God's will.

December 31, 2008

Before I place this diary, I will pray for Sybille's mission and her world.

Sybille has a choice and a destiny.

My destiny is now fulfilled.

I gave my parents hugs that will carry me through any darkness and I'm hopeful to see them again.

SYBILLE'S ADDENDUM

Before going to press, Eston discovered something in Global Good's historical record that astonished him.

It was several passages by Cardinal Patrick Murphy, who we believe to be Blair's parish priest.

He wrote a series of books on the life of Saint Blair Carlisle. The scanned torn passages are few and vague.

Eston believes Good encrypted what they included in their dogma.

What little Eston could ascertain, was that Blair led a resistance within The Apostasy and freed many from the cult's bondage.

Good saw her faith and conviction as worthy of emulation and *they* the deity that could bring a world of divided sects together under one harmonious order.

Which makes sense why Blair kept Father Murphy inside the church when Sister Jo was outside during the demon swarm.

Sister Jo's possession and departure from the religious life were the reason Blair joined The Apostasy!

And Blair saved Father Murphy on the same day at the urging of St. Michael.

Michael had her write the vision to help me reverse what Blair influenced!

Blair was the model of Global Good's initial mission to create unity.

But we still don't know what happened to her.

Eston said if Blair appears to me as an innocent faithful girl, I should trust that is all I am to know.

Because Eston said, "we don't want to invite a serpent into our garden."

BLAIR'S VISION

A woman whose name means Oracle has many gifts. Yet she has no belief in herself.

Her world is overpopulated and Oracle's focus is quota.

Quota means praise. Quota means approval.

Oracle exceeds quota.

Yet Oracle is invisible as are her peers who meet and exceed quota.

Quota means all receive a fair portion of the total contribution.

However, production must increase.

The overpopulated coexist in spaces not their own and eat what they're fed, wear what they're allocated and sleep as they're scheduled.

On the day that Oracle doesn't meet quota, the machines grind to a halt.

Darkness prevails.

She doesn't understand disruption.

Yet, the Suzerain does nothing.

She searches for something to replace the loss.

Rations begin.

The window of judgment is open.

Clouds drape her and gold flecks lure her. She tries to grasp the gold, but her knees are weak and she is bleeding.

She fails.

Oracle fears the Suzerain, though she's not been threatened.
She needs to find the treasure within.
But the treasure resists.
The treasure will only release if a shift occurs, not before.
Time is limited.
Oracle's treasure is the world's salvation.
Below the surface are layers of beings both alive and dead as well as in the final abyss.
The House of Monsters know where knowledge grows.
Her treasure is a curse to the monsters who have fallen into the abyss of their own free will.
Suzerain learns of Oracle's treasure when a great pillar of hope is raised.
The pillar calls upon angelic warriors to protect Oracle and Suzerain's people.
A thousand tongues chatter and their cries fill the air.
She hears their upstretched voices.
Confusion and deception stir the masses.
But Oracle understands angelic speak!
All are under attack from within and without.
They fight one another as well as the monsters.
Oracle's people are eaten with infection.
The monsters are conjoined human and animal.
Oracle knows how to release the human from the animal demons.
Oracle calls the angelic warrior to bring his heavenly comrades to her defense.
He tells her that only she can call the Battle!
Survivors will be few.
Oracle, whose name they'll know on the Day of Awakening, will lead believers to the lamb and peace will return to earth.
Oracle's triumph will restore the covenant established by her ancestors.
Then the abyss will close.
She will be forever remembered as Battlefield.

ACKNOWLEDGMENTS

First, thanks to Ellen Williams for her patience and care in editing books in the St. Blair series as well as other works. I am FOREVER grateful!

A HUGE thanks to Caitlin Poley for beta reading the rough draft of this book. Your sense of urgency and help made the final process tolerable. I struggled with this book. Cutting 10,000 words.

To Lisa DeSpain, I appreciate your help with the cover design, as well as the formatting of my print and digital books, and most recently for promoting me on your marketing site: www.book-2bestseller.com.

To Autumn Brooks of fandommonthlymagazine.blogspot.com thanks for keeping in touch. To Suleika Santana, Soleil Santana, Nathan Santana and all the St. Blair superfans, your enthusiasm is uplifting! God bless you all.

To my brother Mark, who gave me his honest appraisal of the first book, I love and appreciate your feedback more than you know.

To Jennifer Bashoor, Lori Garside, Kim Salter, Marcia Engle, Bunny Cates and Robyn Fairbanks and all the wonderful folks I have met at recent conventions and events, I appreciate your continued interest in the series. It makes the work rewarding to know you await the next book with shared anticipation.

To my daughters, Blair and Marquel, thanks for all the encouragement and love you share with our family and others. I am proud to be your mom. To my husband, Tom, thanks for being my best friend.

ABOUT THE AUTHOR

Emily Skinner lives in Tampa Bay, Florida with her husband, Tom. In addition to writing, she also enjoys selling advertising, traveling, and working with their daughters, Marquel Skinner and Blair Skinner on their film and acting projects. A few of her daughters' projects include: www.anamead.com starring Marquel Skinner and www.theforgottenprincess.com co-created and directed by Blair Skinner.

E.W. Skinner
Young Adult titles:
St. Blair: Children of the Night—Book 1
St. Blair: Sybille's Reign—Book 2
The Diary of St. Blair—Book 3

Emily W. Skinner
Adult: Romantic Suspense titles:
Marquel
Marquel's Dilemma
Marquel's Redemption—coming soon

Memoir
Master of the roman noir

Nonfiction
Emily Millikan Blair—Diary of my Quaker grandmother
(coming soon)

You may reach Emily by writing to:

Emily W. Skinner
PO Box 8590
Seminole, FL 33775-8590

Author events & announcements
www.ewskinner.com
www.emilyskinnerbooks.com
http://thefilmmom.blogspot.com/
www.twitter.com/emilyauthor
www.facebook.com/stblairchildrenofthenight
www.facebook.com/emilyskinnerbooks
www.goodreads.com/author/show/6982753.Emily_W_Skinner
Reviews appreciated!

www.ingramcontent.com/pod-product-compliance
Lightning Source LLC
Chambersburg PA
CBHW071004120726
47910CB00004B/1371